HAUNTED
love

J.L. HINDS
C. L. LEDFORD

Copyright © 2024 by J. L. Hinds & C. L. Ledford

All rights reserved.

No part of this publication may be reproduced, distributed, or transmitted in any form or by any means, including photocopying, recording, or other electronic or mechanical methods, without the prior written permission of the publisher, except as permitted by U.S. copyright law.

The story, all names, characters, and incidents portrayed in this production are fictitious. No identification with actual persons (living or deceased), places, buildings, and products is intended or should be inferred.

Book Cover by Getcovers

First edition 2024

Content Warning

Mentions of depression
Sexual content
Loss of Parents
Death and Gore
Pregnancy (end of book)

Contents

1. Chapter One   1
2. Chapter Two   11
3. Chapter Three   27
4. Chapter Four   38
5. Chapter Five   50
6. Chapter Six   60
7. Chapter Seven   76
8. Chapter Eight   86
9. Chapter Nine   90

10.	Chapter Ten	97
11.	Chapter Eleven	106
12.	Chapter Twelve	122
13.	Chapter Thirteen	132
14.	Chapter Fourteen	140
15.	Chapter Fifteen	150
16.	Chapter Sixteen	162
17.	Chapter Seventeen	172
18.	Chapter Eighteen	181
19.	Chapter Nineteen	192
20.	Chapter Twenty	203
21.	Epilogue	212
Also By C.L. Ledford		216
About C. L. Ledford		218
Also By J. L. Hinds		220
About J. L. Hinds		221

Chapter One

GEORGINNA

I hate my life. All I see when I look around is that everyone I know seems to have love in their life. I'm the only dumbass that doesn't seem to be interested in anyone. I mean, let's get real. No man I've met so far has really piqued my interest. They've just been some jackass who wants to *hit it and quit it*, or they were some clingy weirdo.

None have shown any type of commitment and swept me off my feet. I know that's having pretty high standards, but hell, if they're worthy to earn my respect, they'll earn my love, too.

I *did*, however, once have love, a soulmate. I thought it could last, but unfortunate circumstances took him away from me far too soon.

It all started at Point Break Bar on Interstate 89. We were driving wherever the road took us.

"We haven't seen a single stop for miles. I'm starving, and I need to use the bathroom." I look around, and all I see are trees and overgrown fields. Not a single car or building in sight. I look over at Langdon. Studying his features, the way his long, chestnut hair is slicked back and the almost full beard covering his jaw makes him look so rugged and gives off a lumberjack vibe; I love it! His emerald-green eyes scan the road and beyond. How did I get so lucky to end up with an incredibly sexy man?

"According to the GPS, we should come across a stop in two miles," he says as I lay my head back and stare out of the window, looking at the trees as we pass. It's so beautiful around here. The leaves are amazing: crimson; juniper, and gold. It's so clearly autumn. The weather so far has not been so bad .

I don't know why we took this route.

Although it's picturesque, there's nothing here. We start slowing, and I observe Langdon, then I follow his line of sight. A cottage-looking building appears in the distance. As we get closer, I realize it's a bar. I sit up in my seat, filled with elation to finally seeing a building, but it's a bar, no less. Just the thing I need.

"We'll stop here and eat, then we need to hit the road. We still have a long drive ahead of us, and we need to get there before dark." Langdon explains as we park.

"Fine with me. As long as they have a clean bathroom, good food, and a strong drink, I'll be just fine."

As soon as I walk through the door, I head straight for the bathroom. Langdon grabs my arm, stopping me. "Not so fast. What do you want?"

"Get me a glass of Chardonnay and a chicken sandwich, if they got it."

Following the restroom signs, I turn the corner. "Ugh,"

There's a fucking line. Well, on the plus side, it's not too long, so I guess I'll have to grin and bear it.

I get into the line, and a man stumbles into me. He's wearing a black hood, so I can't quite make out his appearance.

"You better watch your back..." he starts with a deep, gravelly tone. "You'll get what you've got comin' to ya." Without another word, he walks away, leaving me standing here. Stunned.

What the fuck was that?!

Suddenly, I don't need to use the bathroom anymore. I practically ran back to Langdon.

"I don't know if I want to stay here much longer," I rush out as I get to the security of the bar, my anxiety spiking. He looks at me and tilts his head to the side, a *v* forming between his eyebrows. I swear it's so damn hot when he does that; it almost makes me forget what happened.

"Why? What happened?" He wraps his arm around my shoulder and waits for me to respond. I look toward the restrooms and then back at him.

"A man came up to me and told me I had better watch my back and that I was going to get what was coming to me. I don't think I've ever met that man before in my life. I'm scared, Lang." Pulling me in tighter, he presses my head to his well-toned chest. I breathe in his scent. I should figure out a way to bottle that up; it's intoxicating.

"Don't worry about it, Georgie, I'm sure it's just some nut confusing you with someone else. Just stick with me. I'll make sure no one has a chance to go near you." His words do the same trick they've always done and instantly calm me.

"So, when we get to Mount Baker, where will we stay? I know I want to be there for a few days to really enjoy the scenery." I've never been that far north, but I've heard great things about the breathtaking volcanoes there.

I've lived in the small town of Hobart, Oklahoma, my entire life, and I've never been able to explore much, so when Langdon came up with the idea to take the summer to travel, I was more than ready. So far, we've been to Denver, Colorado, where I rode a horse through the trails. It was a beautiful sight. Then we headed south toward Grand Staircase-Escalante National Monument, where we took pictures of gorgeous waterfalls and the canyon. After leaving there, we ended up on a long stretch of road with no buildings in sight. Luckily, we found a spot just in time. I'm not sure how much longer I could've lasted without a bathroom.

"I booked us a cabin in Glacier called Mount Baker Rim. It's got spectacular views of the volcano. I just want the best for you." He winks at me. My cheeks warm at his playful tone. Wrapping my arms around his neck, I kiss him, savoring his lips on mine. His kiss sends shockwaves through my body and has me wanting more.

"Ahem," the bartender disrupts our kiss. "I'm sorry to interrupt this love fest you've got going on here, but here are your drinks." He leans in closer, making me feel uncomfortable. "Also, there's a guy over there that looks like he's fixing to come this way. He's been staring at you, and frankly, it's a little creepy. I figured I'd warn ya." The hair on the back of my neck stands on end.

I take a deep breath and start to turn. Langdon grabs my shoulders and stops me. "Do not look. That'll give him what he wants. Just ignore him."

"What if he's the same one who threatened me?" I can't keep the terror from my voice. I don't want either of us to die today.

"I'll keep you safe no matter what happens. No one will mess with you as long as I'm around." He puts his strong arms around me, and I immediately feel safer. I'm afraid of something happening to him, though. I don't want to lose him. It would devastate me.

"Look, our food is here. We'll take it to-go and be on our way. Drink your wine, you don't want to waste it," Langdon tries to comfort me as he sits on the stool. I usually like to take my time, savor my wine and enjoy the taste, but now I feel the need to chug it down to get out of this crazy bar. Langdon asks the bartender for boxes before suddenly standing and facing away from the bar.

My heart pounds, and I feel like the breath was just taken out of me. I'm too worried to turn around. Afraid I might find that man standing there with a weapon of some sort.

"What do you want from us?" Langdon asks from behind me. The man must've come closer and gotten his attention.

"You've got nothin' to do with this. Mind ya own business," the man spits back. From the sounds of it, he's a lot closer, nearly behind me. I can feel his gaze burning into the back of my head.

Out of curiosity, I turn around—the need to know what's going on eating at me. Immediately,

I regret the decision. The man moves forward, his black hood down, his face clearly shown. I still don't recognize him. What problem does *he* have with *me*? I don't even know who he is. A scar runs from his hairline down to the left corner of his mouth. Gray eyes bore into me.

Langdon stands by my side, slightly in front of me, prepared to defend me if the threat comes any closer. The man stands still, staring at me murderously. My insides run frigid, dread filling every pore in my body. Suddenly, the man lifts a gun, aiming it at me.

Langdon steps in front of me just in time for the gun to go off. The bullet hits him, and he collapses, crumpling on the floor with blood pooling around him.

"No! Langdon!" I fall to my knees at his side. I cover the hole in his stomach, trying desperately to stop the bleeding. "You can't leave me! You hear me?" Tears fall from my eyes as I look up to see the gunman pinned to the ground by bystanders. With my heart aching, I look back at Langdon, lean in, and kiss him. I need him to be okay. "Someone call an ambulance!" I shriek, then I'm grabbed by the arms and forced to my feet.

No! No! I can't leave him!

"Let me go! I need to be with him. He needs medical attention. Do you not see that?! He's dying!" They don't seem to hear me as I struggle in the person's arms. Before I know it, I'm in mine and Langdon's car, thrown in the back with the fucking child safety latch on.

"What are you doing?! I need to be with him. Let me go!" I kick and scream, trying to get back to Lang.

He's my world. I'm not leaving without him.

The tall, blond, muscular assailant grabs my legs with one hand and takes his belt off with the other. *Damn, he's strong.* I struggle so hard to get out of his grasp but to no avail. Dread washes over me. I don't need this right now. Please don't tell me he's not going to have his way with me.

"Settle down. This is just to keep you still." He explains as he fastens the belt around my legs. A mixture of relief and terror fills me, he is not going to take advantage of me. On the other hand, he's got me tied so I can't move. That's not going to stop me. I struggle as much as I can, wriggling and scrabbling in any way I can.

"What do you want from me!?" I ask, trying to appeal to any humanity this man may have.

"I want to take you away from here. There are things here you don't understand. It's too dangerous for you out here. I can take you south, as far as I can go, but you must go home before you wind up like your boyfriend." He sets my feet down, puts the seat belt on me, closes the door, and gets in the driver's seat. I can't believe this is happening! The love of my life has been taken from me. I'm being forced to leave him here in the middle of nowhere.

Laying my forehead on the cool window, I stare at the bar and my soulmate moves further out of sight. I'm numb to the world.

What am I going to do now? How can I live without the one thing that gave my life meaning?

Chapter Two

GEORGINNA

One Year Later

"Come on, Gina. It's almost been a year. You have to go out and have some fun. You can't sulk around all the time. It's not healthy." My friend Gracie has been trying to convince me to go on a road trip with her and Charlie for a few days now. I really don't feel up to it. Since losing Lang, I can't get myself to take another road trip. That was the one and only time I will leave Hobart.

"I can't, Gracie. The one occasion I leave Oklahoma, I lose my world. I can't do it. I can't lose anyone else. I'm sorry. We can go out, but we have to stay around here." I cross my arms as I sit on the couch in my living room.

Ever since Langdon was shot, I've been sliding in a downward spiral. Luckily, I still have my apartment, thanks to my best friend, Gracie Lancaster. She became my roommate to help with rent. Then her boyfriend Charlie moved in. They have been so helpful. I wouldn't have made it much further without them.

"Listen, Georginna," Charlie begins, sitting beside me. "You had a pretty traumatic experience, and I get that, but you can't let that get in the way of having a life. Okay, listen, how about you think of this road trip as a way of honoring his memory. You guys weren't able to make it to Mount Baker, right?" Taking a deep steadying breath, I bite my bottom lip and nod. "Well, how about we take that trip in honor of Langdon. We can pin ribbons in his memory."

I kinda like that idea, but I'm still not so sure I'm ready. Gracie sits on the other side of me and takes my hand in hers. She gives me the look she knows I hate most, pity. "Do it for Lang. He would want you to. Before you guys left for the trip, he told me how excited he was to take you there. To show you things that you've only dreamed of. He wanted to give you the world" She takes a deep breath and leans in closer. "Listen, I shouldn't tell you this, but he also told me that if, God forbid, anything were to happen, to make sure you were able to experience everything. He wanted you to be happy, Gina." Tears stream from my eyes as I listen to her words. My heart breaking again.

She wraps me in her arms as the overwhelming grief surrounds me. I can't believe this. Did he know he was going to die? Why didn't he tell me? Why did he have to leave me? It's almost been a year, and it's still getting to me. I take a deep, steadying breath.

"We'll have to take a different route. I am *not* going the same way. It would be too hard." Reluctantly, I agree as I sit up. Gracie hands me a box of tissues that I conveniently have on the side table for the long nights thinking about Lang, and I wipe the wetness from my eyes and cheeks. In the past few months, I've managed to get a job and try to live some semblance of a life.

I went on a couple of dates, but none went any further than a first meeting due to the egocentric jackasses who just wanted to hit it and quit it. I've never felt the same as I did with him. It was going well until Gracie and her boyfriend mentioned going on a road trip, then the memory of that day came flooding back.

Gracie smiles and stands. "That's great! Of course we'll take a different route. The route you took sounds deserted. We'll take a scenic route so we can take pictures and make frequent stops if we have to." She squeezes my shoulder and heads to her room; I assume to start packing.

"I'm so glad you've changed your mind. This'll be good for you to get out and explore," Charlie adds as he gets up and goes to help Gracie.

Looking at the picture of Langdon and me at the waterfall in Utah, sitting on the table next to the couch, I confess. "I don't know if I can do this, Lang. What if I were to get into the same situation? This time, you won't be there to save me." *I guess that wouldn't be too bad. I can use this to honor what we had.* I blow a kiss to him and head to my room. *Maybe this trip won't be so bad.*

We're eleven hours into our trip, and we've made it to Jamestown, Wyoming. I don't want to jinx things, but so far, it's been going pretty well. We've been to so many places already. The first hour, my anxiety started to spike. It wasn't until we were about three hours in that I was finally able to calm down.

"Anyone want to use the bathroom?" Charlie chirps when we pull up to a gas station pump. "I need to get gas anyway."

That wouldn't be a terrible idea.

I open the door and head toward the bathroom. A person bumps into me from behind. My anxiety rises again. *NO! This cannot be happening again!* Why does this always seem to happen to me? On the anniversary of Lang's death, no less.

My heart races as I slowly turn, hoping to be able to make my escape before anything happens. It's not like they could actually do anything to me since we're in a public place. There are more witnesses this time. Also, we're in the middle of a town, and police officers have to be nearby.

Turning, I'm met by an older man, who seems to be in his fifties or sixties. "I'm sorry, my dear, I didn't mean to bump into you…" he starts as he takes off his glasses and wipes them off with his shirt. "These things get so dirty sometimes, I can hardly see through them." He lifts his glasses to the ceiling and looks through them before putting them back on.

"That's okay," I respond, relieved that it was a case of mistaken identity. Offering him a smile, I resume my path to the bathroom.

I can't believe I got all worked up over a simple mistake. *I need to relax and enjoy the rest of this trip.*

I lean against the window and lay my head against the coolness it provides as I stare at the road zipping by on our way to Mount Baker. Thoughts of Lang come to mind…

"Is this seat taken?" I look up to see the most mesmerizing emerald-green eyes looking back at me. His hand rests on the chair beside me at the bar. I like to come here to the new Book Bar that just opened

in our town. It's a place I come to drink and read. Others are here to gather in their book clubs and drink, discussing what they are currently reading.

"Have at it," *I say with a smile, waving to the empty seat beside me.*

"So, what brings you here, besides the obvious?" *he asks, gesturing toward the books with his thumb and then at the bar.*

"This is the newest hottest place in town. Books and booze, what could be better? You?"

"I just moved to town and found this place. It looked interesting enough, so I figured I'd try it out. I'm glad I did because I got to meet the most gorgeous woman I've ever seen." *Heat rises to my cheeks. This man sure knows how to make a woman blush. He doesn't look so bad, either.*

"Where'd you move from?" *I've got to know more about this incredibly sexy man. He seems to be interested in me, and I'm definitely attracted to him in every way.*

"First of all, my name is Langdon, and I'm from Port Lions, Alaska. I wanted a change of scenery. I got tired of living in a frigid small town. My family's actually from here, so I wanted to get to know my roots." *Wow, an Alaskan man. I've only met men from around here or the south; I've never met any from up north. He's nothing like I expected. He is the type you'd think would live in the woods. His brown hair, shaved on the sides and long on top. His look gives off a lumberjack vibe. The only thing that is different is the fact that his beard is trimmed.*

He turns toward me and places his arm on the back of his chair. "So, you have a boyfriend?"

I smile, thrown by his forward question. "No..." I smile, not knowing what else to say. He grins in return. Before I know it, he reaches forward and wraps his hand around the back of my head, pulling me closer. I close my eyes on instinct as our lips touch. His soft lips caressing mine. Holy fuck, he tastes like heaven.

When we finally come up for air, Langdon lays his forehead on mine. "Oh, my fuck." His eyes remain closed as we sit there, catching our breath. Something inside me wants to take him home and have my way with him. What is wrong with me? We literally just met, and I already want him to devour me.

I lift my head and look at him. His eyes mirroring the hunger I feel. Normally, I like to take things slowly and get to know each other first, but right now, none of that matters.

"Do you want to go to my place?" he asks huskily.

Unable to help myself, I jump off the stool "Yes," I breathe a little too quickly, before we pay the bill and head out the door. "Hold on." I pause as we walk out the door. "What car are we taking?" I ask, turning to him.

"Where are you parked?" He looks around at the cars parked along the street. "I parked there. There wasn't any room out here, and I wanted it covered and protected." I point to the parking garage across the street.

Langdon smiles and scoops me up in his arms. "Great! I'm parked right here, so we'll take mine." He kisses me hard, and when we get to his car, he sets me on my feet next to the passenger side of his car. Opening the door for me, he takes my hand, helping me in. Such a gentleman.

My lust for him grows stronger with every second that passes. He opens the driver's side door, climbs in, and we head to his house, my patience thinning by the minute.

Langdon sets his hand on my thigh, igniting the fire in my middle. He rubs the inside of my thigh.

Oh, that feels so good. His hand slowly roams higher until he's touching my sex through my jeans. I so badly want him to take me here and now, but I'll take what I can get. I lean my head back and enjoy the sensations that hit when his pinky hits the right spot.

"Mmm..." He doesn't stop, moving faster until I'm tightly gripping the seat. Fuck, that feels so good, the tension building, telling me I'm close. Just as I'm about to orgasm, he stops. I open my eyes and look at him incredulously.

"Why'd you stop?" I ask as I try to steady my breathing. A chuckle escapes his lips as he puts the car in park. I look around. "We're here," he answers as he hurries out of the car, opens my door, and helps me out.

He scoops me up in his strong arms, and we head to his home. Glancing around, I admire the surroundings. He actually has a house. I pictured him living in an apartment since he said he just moved here. Don't focus on the surroundings, *a voice in my head that I don't recognize chimes in. I turn back toward Langdon and nuzzle into his neck. I kiss just under his ear, and he growls seductively. I love the way he tastes. I can't get enough of him.*

Langdon opens the door with ease as we make our way to his room. He sets me on my feet. I've never felt this kind of heat before. It's so different. I feel as though we're meant for each other. Like we've known each other forever. He brings my body to his and kisses me with fervor, his hand on the small of my back. Then, both of his hands travel down to my ass, squeezing. I savor every ounce of his kiss. Dear Lord, he makes me feel things I never thought possible. How am I falling so hard so fast?

I grab the back of his neck and deepen the kiss, our tongues dancing in rhythm. He picks me up, and I wrap my legs around his waist. He lays me on the bed, his mouth never leaving mine. He kisses my neck just under my ear. Oh, my fuck! I feel that all the way down to my core. "Mmmm...." I moan. Shit, he hasn't even touched me yet, and my body feels like it's on fire.

His hand reaches up underneath my T-shirt, reaching under my bra, cupping my breast. The pleasure increases as he flicks the pink bud between his fingers.

He trails kisses down my neck, moving his fingers south, kisses following every touch. "Oh God, Langdon!" I say breathlessly as my fingers find his hair.

He unbuttons my jeans and slides them down, kissing as he goes, stopping just long enough to remove my shoes, socks, and finally my jeans.

He kneels between my legs, resting his hands on my ankles. A mischievous grin appears on his face, telling me he's up to no good, then slowly, achingly slowly brings his hands closer and closer, rubbing up my legs until he reaches the apex of my thighs. My body igniting with every second of his touch. He finally reaches his target and presses my clit with the pad of his thumb. Inserting two fingers inside me, he thrums and pumps his fingers at the same speed. I grab the sheets, feeling the orgasm creeping closer.

"Oh, Gahhhh... Mmmm" I moan on the edge. Grabbing his broad shoulders. He removes his fingers; his hot breath takes their place. His tongue laps at my clit, bringing me higher and higher until I can't stand it. I feel the orgasm building. It's just there in touching distance, but it won't let go. It lingers, I wish it would fucking let go already. Just as I'm on the precipice, he lifts his head, stopping. I open my eyes and look down at him. Eyes wide. "Why'd you stop?! I was so close!" My voice sounding gruff and a little whiny.

He smiles, crawling up my body, kissing my heated body as he goes, making my body jolt with each touch of his lips until he reaches my mouth. Kissing me before standing at the foot of the bed.

He quickly removes his shoes before taking his pants completely off. I look down, and my eyes widen at the massive bulge poking out of his boxers. Holy shit! He's huge! *I sit up, crawling toward him, needing to taste him. I hook my fingers in the waistband of his boxers, and then I look up to find he's staring at me with hunger in his eyes, a look I am all too familiar with. I smile, a naughty idea springing to mind. As slow as I can manage, I pull his boxers down, staring at him. Licking my lips the entire time,, wanting to drive him as crazy as he's driven me. My nails leave their mark as I go.*

Langdon's hard cock springs out, and I'm tempted to put him in my mouth, but I need to focus on the task at hand. Once I have his boxers off, I run my nails ever so slowly up his legs, causing a low growl to escape his mouth.

"Oh God, Georgie! What are you doing to me?"

Suddenly, he lifts me, throws me on the bed, crawls on top of me, and dominates me with his mouth. I savor every bit of him. A low growl escapes him, and something inside me starts to stir.

He grabs the hem of my shirt and lifts it from me in one swoop. Next with one hand, he undoes the clasp of my bra, releasing my breasts. He proceeds to remove his own, revealing a sexy-as-hell body, toned and tan with a tattoo on his left pec of a tribal paw, writing circling it. He throws his shirt to the side and grabs both of my wrists with one hand, pinning them above my head. His lips land on mine with fervor. The tip of his cock teasing my folds, rubbing against my clit. Shit, that feels so good.

I move my hips up, trying desperately to get him inside me, but he continues his torture. Leaning down, close enough that I can feel his hot breath surrounding my ear. "So hungry, aren't we?" *he whispers, causing me to whimper. A growl escapes his lips as he puts me out of my misery, slamming into me.*

"Fuck, Langdon!" *I scream his name in pleasure. He continues to pound into me, my ecstasy growing higher and higher until I climax. Langdon stiffens, his cock swelling and pulsing inside me. He collapses on top of me, kissing my neck. He pulls out of me, making my body jolt. He lays beside me as we cuddle, trying to steady our breathing.* "I love you, Georgie."

Although we just met, I can't help but feel the same way.

"I love you too, Lang"

When we first met, I felt more than just a sexual attraction to Lang. I was drawn to him in every way. For weeks after that, we felt such a hunger for one another that was beyond anything I've ever experienced. After he died, a piece of me died with him. Nothing has ever felt the same.

I glance around, this place seems eerily familiar. "Where are we?" I ask, looking at nothing but trees and overgrown fields.

Gracie glances at the GPS. "Looks like we're on Highway 287 heading north. We made it to Wyoming."

My heart starts to beat harder and faster. I can't breathe. "Pull over!" I shout. As soon as we do, I leap from the car.

"Georgie, What's wrong?!" Gracie jumps out after me, kneeling at my side as I squeeze my chest. I told them I didn't want to go this way. This is the highway that started it all.

We need to go to him! He needs us.

"What?" I ask. Did Gracie just tell me Lang needs us? "I said, what's wrong?" I shake my head. "No, that's not what you said. You said he needs us." She looks at me in confusion. "No, I didn't." I stare at her. I know I'm not going crazy; I can't be. *We are so close to him. I can feel it. He needs us.*

This time, I know I'm going crazy. I heard the voice, but her lips didn't move. I look around. Something captures my attention in the woods. I squint my eyes, and when they adjust, I feel like the breath has been knocked out of me. I have to get closer; I need to know.

I can feel him. It must be him. Mates know. Go to him.

I stand and dart toward the woods with all I can give. I can't think about that voice inside my head. I have to make sure, but it can't possibly be, can it? I get closer, but he seems to be moving further away.

When I get closer, I feel my heart swell.

Can it be? How is he still alive? I watched him die.

Langdon?...

Chapter Three

LANGDON

This will be my first time at the annual Bear Meeting since Garrett brought out my bear. I hate him for trying to kill my woman and then shoot me. Not being able to find her doesn't sit right in my soul. *My Georgie*.

Whoever took her away from me on that fateful day did a good job of hiding her. All that is left of her is the human scent memory of her. Which is fading with each passing day. Agitating the bear inside of me.

For us to be known as solitary animals, we hold plenty of events and meetings to bring us together.

A few of the other males have taken this as a way to find their mates. Although I have so many beautiful females around me, I just want Georgie.

A year ago today, my life changed. Garret was the one to change it. He still won't tell me why he was after Georgie. Like it's some secret. What would a bear want with a human? And how long had he been stalking her? Is he still stalking her?

Leaning against the tree in my human form, I watch the others mingle and talk. I cross my arms over my chest. Garret talks to the Grizzly Bear tribe chief. Technically, he is my chief too, but they both unnerve me. Now I know why my father didn't like the Grizzlies. They do things completely differently from what we do back home.

The sight of Garrett takes me back to that day a year ago...

Excruciating pain rips through my torso as the red-hot bullet lodges in my abdomen. I hit the floor, and Georgie's face floats in my vision as it starts to blur. Tears streaming down her cheeks as she is pulled from my side.

The man who shot me takes Georgie's place as he squats above me before heaving my body onto his shoulder. As small as he is, he is strong. He opens the SUV's door and places me in the back seat.

"Get back to the territory. And step on it." I desperately try to stay conscious, but the last thing that I remember was the man leaning over me. His canines elongated before he sinks them into my shoulder.

I wake to the presence of something else in my head. The bear side of me. It's weird, to say the least. Since it was the last thing that I wanted. While my vision returns to me, I lie in what I can only assume is a hospital bed.

The beeping of the monitors tells me that my heart rate has spiked. No longer my normal sixty-five beats per minute. Glancing over at the monitor, my resting heart rate is now ninety.

But I don't feel like I am running that high. The continuous beating of the monitors causes my heartbeat to race even more in anxiety.

The door opens, and in walks a woman in a white coat. Another bear shifter. But a grizzly, nothing like what I am. They can't know that I'm not one of them.

How did the man shoot me before waking my bear with his bite knowing that I'm not a human?

I sit up in the bed, barely even wincing.

"I'm glad that you are awake. You had a few of us worried. Most unranked bears can't change a human."

"Yeah, well, I guess I'm lucky."

She smiles and checks my vitals. I don't trust her as far as I could throw her, and that's saying something since Kodiaks are the strongest bears of all.

My family is the fiercest and had high hopes that I would remain in the tribal lands to take my place as chief. But I wanted more; I wanted to find my mate.

"All your vitals look good. I'm sure we can get you out of here in the next day or two."

Now, I stand in the back of the meeting. I kept my breed a secret to them. Claiming to be a grizzly since Garrett thought I was a mere human when he shot me. The overwhelming need to find a way away from them to allow my bear to get out and stretch his legs has me fidgeting in place.

Letting him out is hard when my kind are bigger than the chief himself, making him question me about my heritage was the last thing I wanted to do. Anytime the hunting party went out, I made sure to exclude myself. Or I would hunt in my human form. Which I'm still good at.

Garrett's gaze falls over to me and then the Chief. Well, there goes anyway of sneaking away, I think as he motions me over with a flick of his head.

Why do you bend to their will? You are not meant to be like this! We could go home, the voice in my head snarls. He doesn't like how I allow others to tell me what to do. But I'm just playing my part until I can leave.

Because we need to be cautious. We can't let them know about us. Well, we could, but then we won't find our mate again. I'm certain that she is still out there.

Tentatively, I make my way to Garrett and the Chief. As much as I want to leave, the need to find her compels me to stay. Finding Georgie is the only thought I have. I won't be able to find her on my own.

Taking a knee in front of the Chief, I stay put until he motions for me to stand.

"Langdon, Garrett tells me you have been a valuable asset this past year. Why don't you and a few other hunters go and find more food?"

"Of course, Chief. What would your heart desire?" I ask him while staring behind him. My bear wants me to hold his gaze, but I can't do that. It would give us away too soon.

"You know, I would like moose. Bring me back an enormous one."

I bow and turn on my heel. A few younger bears follow me out into the trees. The smell of the forest begs me to shift and let my bear out to run. With these cubs with me, there is no way that can happen. When we stop at the stream, I squat and study the tracks of another predator. The big cat was here moments before us. So he may still be around. Which won't surprise me because why hunt when the bears bring in kills.

"Langdon, man, what's the hold-up?"

Standing, I spot Mikey. The kid drives me insane. He never does anything he's told to do. He's insubordinate, but Chief Mateo keeps him around for some reason.

"Well, considering there is a big cat very close to us, I think we need to be incredibly cautious of it."

He folds his arms and huffs. Turning away from him and sniffing the air. A familiar scent catches my attention but quickly shifts with the wind. Turning back to the others, I size them up.

"Okay, Hank and Collier, go find some berries. Mikey and Nick find some smaller game. Once you've done that, meet me back here." They all nod, other than Mikey, and head off.

I continue down the stream. The chief is crazy to think I could possibly find a moose. Hell, most of them stay together, and I'm not going to put those kids' lives in danger. What makes it worse is that I'm sure they did this on purpose.

Making my way across the passing water, I glance at its reflective surface. My beard had grown out as has my hair, telling me it is time to shave

Can you not let me out now? They are gone. I need my time out in the open, too. You know, the grown bear whimpers in my head. I swear when they assigned him to me, they must have given me a cub.

I know. But I'm not too sure about them being far enough away. We don't need to cause a panic, I answer.

My bear rolls his eyes and plops down on his rear. If we shift, he will make the ground tremble under his weight. Making all the other wildlife scatter.

Listening to the sounds of the wildlife brings me joy in this haunted life. It made me pause in life to remember the good times. Like when I had met Georgie.

Well, that's rude that you don't want me. I feel unloved at the moment.

If you haven't figured it out by now, my bear is very close to his feelings. Which often gives me a crushing headache.

It's not that I didn't want you. I just didn't want to be tied down in our tribe. I needed to get away, and our mate wasn't on our islands, I tell him. It's the truth. Somewhat. I don't like the idea of being a leader. The need to explore to find my calling has always been strong.

Still, could've gone along with the summoning. Now we have to stay here until we can leave without being noticed. I could've allowed them to summon him before I left, but then that would have meant that my parents would know where I am. Like I said, I don't want to be tied down.

Could you be any more of a baby right now? I groan. This bear of mine is a big baby, and for one with so much promise and potential, you'd think I'd get a mature one.

Yes... he answers me with sad eyes.

Sighing, I wade waist deep the rest of the way through the brisk, cool stream. The scent coming to me stronger.

Dipshit! Get your ass in gear! That's our mate!

But that can't be because I couldn't find her when I went out to search for her. Fear rushes through me. What if my almost dying changed things? What if it's not Georgie?

I turn. If it isn't Georgie, I don't want her. This scent isn't anything like Georgie's. I'm not going to whoever this person is. No one can make me.

Langdon?

That voice! But it can't be her. Could it? I turn at that moment to see her standing at the tree line. The sun is setting behind her as the wind tosses her hair around her face.

I start toward her when the sound of the brush rustling and the scent of one of the kids heads my way. Glancing back to Georgie I finally run toward her.

Georgie stands there like I'm a ghost. In her defense, she probably thinks I died. Because she wasn't there when Garrett took me back to the tribe's territory.

Encircling her in my arms, I pull her close to me. Georgie starts to shake as she embraces me back. Her tears land on my bare chest, and I pull her closer.

"Georgie, I need you to get back in that car. I will come to find you. But I need you to get out of here." I push her to arm's length and grab her chin gently but firmly to make her stare up at me.

"But why, Lang? I want to stay here with you," Georgie whines as the tears continue to fall down her cheeks.

"Because I haven't figured out why that man was trying to kill you. So I need you to go, and then I'll find you. Okay?" I hold her face, trying to get her to see reason.

"You need to come with us. He will hurt you too!" Georgie grabs hold of my forearms and tries to drag me with her.

"He's not going to hurt me. Because he has a use for me. Now go! I will find you!"

Georgie tries to keep me from leaving her before Gracie walks to her from the car and wraps her arms around her waist. Dragging her back to the vehicle. I haven't let the tribe know she's alive. I had to protect her. That's my life's purpose.

When Gracie has her safely in the car, I regret not kissing her. To feel her lips on mine again after this long year. I can't believe she would come back to this state. Let alone this road.

"Langdon. We found a moose here. We need your help to take it down." Nick comes up to me, glancing between me and the car now speeding down the road.

"Okay, let's go. It is what the chief wants." I turn from the road and head back into the woods.

There is nothing that would keep me from finding her again. If I have to leave in the dead of night, I will, just to find my mate again.

Chapter Four

Georginna

I breathe in his scent as we embrace. I can't believe it. He's alive! Tears spring in my eyes. Just as my heart starts to mend from knowing Lang is still alive and with me again, I'm ripped away from him. He tells me it's dangerous, that I have to go. I don't want to go. I've just found him. I don't want to be apart from him any longer.

As I'm forced into the car, having to leave the love of my life yet again, I commit his scent to memory along with his words, "I will find you." The last words he spoke to me for God only knows how long.

I lay my head back, and I can't help but smile, knowing he's still around. I haven't completely lost him. "Where are we going, Grace? I don't want to go too far."

"I know Georgie. We're going to Yellowstone as planned. You heard him. It's not safe here. There's still someone who wants you dead. Don't worry. You both will be back together before you know it." I know she's trying her hardest to make me feel better, but I won't until I'm back in Langdon's arms.

I gaze out the window, looking through the trees. Although the sight of the colorful pines, firs, and junipers are amazing, I can't focus on them. I was so close yet so far to the love of my life.

Langdon, I don't know or even think it's possible for you to hear this, but I love you more than you know. We're going to Yellowstone National Park. Please find me so we can be together again.

I know it's a long shot, and I may just be thinking to myself. Perhaps I'm just nuts, but I hope somehow, Lang gets that message and finds his way back to me.

We arrive at Yellowstone, and although I should be happy we made it without incident, I'm numb. Part of me is missing with Lang not around.

"It is so beautiful!" Gracie says as we stand on the bridge, looking out toward the Morning Glory Pool. Gracie and Charlie are in each other's arms, staring out at the amazing sight. The edge of the pool is a shade of amber then fades into spring green then, as the pool deepens, it turns a brilliant sky to royal blue.

Looking up, I stare in the direction I know Lang is. When will he be here? Does he even know where I'm at? He kept saying he'd find me, but I don't see how.

He told us he will find us. You need to trust that he will. I know he will. Who are you? Why can I hear you, but no one else can?

I guess I'll just have to give in to the crazy and talk to this internal being. Maybe it'll get my mind away from thinking about the one thing I need the most.

All in good time. I am a part of you, always have been. I've just been hibernating until the time is right until you found our mate.

Mate?

Do you mean soul mate? Because he's been there for a while, I haven't heard from you until recently.

Now, I'm definitely curious about this voice. What is it? She's obviously a part of my psyche, but why is she just speaking up now?

Not quite 'soul' mate. You will find everything in time. Right now, is not the time.

Gracie walks up beside me and leans on the railing. "I don't understand what's happening, Grace. First, I lost the love of my life. Then, I start having pains followed by words in my head telling me he's near. Finally, I end up finding out Langon's alive, only to be torn away from him again. I don't know how much longer I can live like this. I *have* to find him again and get him back. I'm going crazy without him." Tears start falling as I turn to my best friend. She stands and wraps me in a hug.

"It's great he's alive, but like he said, he wants you to be safe. He needs you to be somewhere he knows you will be away from harm. He *did* say he will find you, and he will. Earlier when we stopped, what did you think I'd said?. Are you hearing voices?"

Shit, does she think I'm going crazy? Why did I have to say anything?

Clearing my throat, I take a deep breath. "No, I'm not hearing voices. With everything going on, I've been feeling off lately, and I thought you said something." I can't just sit around knowing he's alone and in danger.

I need to go find him and help him so he can come back home with me. I know Gracie won't understand. She has her love right here with her. I don't think she quite understands how I feel. I won't be whole until I'm with Langdon again.

We know where he is now. We can follow his scent and rescue him. We must be better prepared for the threat.

I don't know exactly how to prepare for something like that. He said they needed him, so that's the only reason they haven't killed him.

I walk around the gift shop. The atmosphere of the shop gives off a cabin feel. Wooden shelves hold a variety of items such as stuffed animals, candles and trinkets.

While Gracie and Charlie find some sort of memento, I browse for any sort of weapon I can use in case I run into trouble.

There's a slingshot in the corner over there. That's the best thing here, The voice in my head chimes in.

I glance in the right-hand corner, and sure enough there's a slingshot with toy pebbles. That'll have to do. My aim is pretty decent, so this is perfect.

I look over at Gracie and Charlie. They seem to be stuck in their own little love bubble, making my heart ache for Lang.

After paying for the slingshot, I make my way out of the gift shop.

"Gina, where are you going?" Gracie calls after me, right behind me, startling me. Looking around, Charlie is at the register, paying for whatever they have chosen.

"I'm just going to go to the room. I'm tired, and it's been a long trip," I try to sound convincing. I don't need her to know what my plans are tonight.

She gives me a look and takes me by the arm, leading me outside. "Whatever you plan on doing, don't."

I arch my brow, playing dumb. "What do you mean? I'm just going to the room."

She huffs out a breath and crosses her arms. "Gina, I *know* you. Now that you know Lang's alive, you're concocting some elaborate plan to get him back. That's the same kinda stuff you've always done growing up. Your parents wouldn't let you go out, so you would hatch some scheme to leave without them knowing. It never works out. You always got caught, then I had to swoop in and save your sorry ass."

I laugh, just remembering the stuff I tried to pull growing up, but I'm not a kid anymore. I *know* what I'm doing, and I'll be better prepared for whatever is thrown my way.

I take a deep breath and give in. "Ok, fine. Maybe I *do* have something planned. Can you blame me? What if it was Charlie? Would you just sit idly by knowing he's alive and in danger?"

Her face softens, and she grabs my hands in hers. "I know I don't know what you're going through, and yes, I would *want* to do something, but Gina, it's too dangerous. We're talking about people who tried to kill you. They almost killed Langdon. There's no telling what they'll do to you if they find you." There's no talking her into being okay with me doing what I must.

"Fine, I won't go," I relent. She smiles and takes a breath. I didn't realize she had been so tense, but she seems to relax more. "Great! Let's go check out the rest of the park. There's so much to discover here."

We're not going to really just sit by, right? the voice in my head asks.

Of course not, He needs us... me.

Great, now I'm referring to this entity as a separate part of me.

"What's so funny?" Gracie asks, smiling.

"Nothing, I was just thinking about Langdon and the jokes that he told me."

When Gracie nods, I feel a little guilty for lying to her, but she wouldn't understand. She'll probably think I'm going crazy.

After dark, I grab my slingshot and throw away the toy pebbles. All I need is this slingshot. If I time it right, I can nail someone with a sharp rock.

When I was a kid, I had one and I was a pretty good shot with it. I ended up shooting holes straight through glass bottles. The trick is to aim and draw back as far as you can. That way, the missile will fly faster and land a harder punch.

Sneaking past Gracie and Charlie's room, I use the compass and map on my phone to try and find Langdon. Making it to the road, I figure which way is south. I *do* remember we were headed north when I *Don't worry, I have you covered. When we get close, I'll sense him.*

Good to know. I walk along the edge of the woods, making sure to stay out of sight. I can't help but think of my time with Lang. We've had a lot of crazy moments that I keep with me.

I cut through the woods, trying to be as stealthy as possible. Needing to catch my breath, I lean against the tree. Holy hell, I am so unfit. I need to work out more.

So... What's the plan when we get there? We haven't really gone over what we'll do once we get to where they have him, the voice in my head says as I take a rest.

I don't know. I was going to play it by ear and figure it out as I go.

Well, she does have a point. What will I do? When I said his name, he seemed to hear me and turned, running toward me. What if I do the same and call to him?

Okay, this is what we're going to do...

"Shit." I look down at my phone, and it's dead.

Well that's just fucking fantastic. Everything looks the same. I don't even know which way I came from. *I should've brought a compass or something or at least made sure my phone was charged.*

I take a shot in the dark and continue forward. Maybe I'll get lucky and get back on track. Leaves start rustling. That doesn't sound like just the wind. I duck behind the tree, trying to make myself as small as possible.

I cock my head to the side and listen carefully. It sounds like heavy steps. I close my eyes, hoping it's dark enough that whoever, or whatever it is, won't see me. The sound gets closer, and my heart rate accelerates.

Please just go away.

Yeah, asking nicely will do the trick, the voice chides.

Will you hush? I don't need the disembodied voice talking to me when I'm trying to concentrate on not getting caught, or worse, killed.

The rustling and stomping gets closer. I sit straight up against the tree.

GRRRR.

The huff and growl of an animal sounds behind me. By the sounds of it, it's huge. Suddenly, I'm grabbed from behind.

Shit, shit, shit! As I open my eyes, they widen, and a terrified scream escapes me, a sound I don't quite recognize.

I stare in terror at a grizzly bear, I look into its cold, black eyes. This can't be happening! It holds me to its side as it turns, heading where it came from.

GRRRRRR.

Turning my head, I spot a much bigger bear charging from the right. As it gets closer, the grizzly holding me drops me and stands defensively, ready to fight

I take it these two aren't friends.

That's what you think in this situation?! Focus. You have two hotties fighting over you, she offers..

What the hell are you talking about? You're talking as though you're attracted to them. They may be fighting over me to see which one kills me. I feel her rolling her eyes.

Okay, this is getting weird. Now, I'm starting to sense her as a different person inside of me.

I glance up to find the bears entangled. The bigger bear swings its massive paw at the grizzly claws extended as it leaves deep, and bloody grooves carved into its opponent's chest. The grizzly falls with a thud. I can't tell whether it's unconscious or dead.

I look back up at the big bear as it stalks toward me. Fearful, I scoot back as fast as I can, but not fast enough as it scoops me up. The last thing I see before everything fades to black is emerald-green eyes.

Chapter Five

LANGDON

We don't have any luck in getting the moose. Mikey wasn't capable of doing what was needed to get it down and dispatch it quickly. I swear if I had a dollar for every big game animal he has made us lose. I wouldn't have to be here right now.

If you would shift you could make him submit to you. Then, he would do what you wanted him to do.

Not now. I roll my eyes at my bear. One minute, he is being a baby, and the next, he is acting like he is the top bear.

After returning to the meeting and passing all the meat and berries to the tribe chief, I wait for it to turn dark before leaving in search of Georgie. The only thing I can hope for is that she will wait for me to find her. Because I have yet to find out why this tribe wants her dead.

Georgie is human, so I can't wrap my mind around why they want her gone. I mean, humans often made bad decisions, but she hadn't ever been out this way before our trip. So, why the deadly attack? They have to have mistaken her for someone else.

Or you could be missing something. I mean, you've missed things before. I swear this bear of mine drives me insane most days.

Getting to the edge of the territory line, I spot one of the other bears walking his patrol route. I wait until he passes me before I catch her scent. My heart rate speeds up when his head snaps to her scent on the wind. I sneak over to my right, trying to get him from behind.

What are you doing? He is going to get our mate, my bear growls at me. I roll my eyes. He can be a little out there sometimes.

I know what I'm doing. I've watched this bear fight, and he's sloppy. When my bear was summoned, they put me in the ring with him. As a child growing up in my tribe, I was taught to fight and defend myself without my bear. So, taking him down with my bear would be easy, but that isn't going to happen.

I come back around the tree and shift into my bear. It has been a long time since I was able to shift. And it is amazing to be standing at my almost ten-foot height. Dan has a hold of Georgie, his claws lengthening. The rage I feel as she struggles to get out of his grasp fuels my need to get to her.

When Dan sees me coming, he doesn't recognize me. I make sure to never shift in front of any of them. As I get close to him, he drops Georgie, and I stand on my back legs. The roar from the other bear freezes Georgie in fear, her heart beating rapidly in her chest.

I roar back at him, and he charges me, locking us in the tussle. Using my teeth, I tear his ear, shredding it to pieces. Dan uses his claws to dig into my left arm, scoring it to the muscle.

The good thing about being a shifter, is that we heal faster than normal people and bears. So it isn't something to worry about. Killing a shifter is possible, but you have to take out the head or the heart. Most of the time, though, it isn't that easy.

Bringing my arm back, I swing, hitting Dan right in his face. The deep grooves in his chest are bright red in the night sky. Dan drops to the ground, his weight making the earth rumble.

I fall to all fours and stalk over to where Georgie is huddling against the tree. Scooping her up in my arms, I allow my eyes to connect with hers while my bear permits me to shift back.

Georgie faints in my arms, and I glance around before running to the only place that will keep her safe. There is no way that I'm going to take her to my home in the tribe. The only other place no one else knows about is the cave further in the woods.

It's a long walk with Georgie's light weight in my arms. But I wouldn't have it any other way.

Reaching the cave, I lay her on the moss and fern bedding. Quickly making a fire to keep her warm, I kiss her temple and then leave her to get back to Dan.

By the time I get back, someone is already kneeling over him. At first, I don't recognize who it is until they stand and stalk to me.

Why the fuck would Gracie be out here?

"Where is she!" I notice her eyes flicker between her normal eye color to a golden one. That's interesting.

"You must be the other scent all over Georgie. Why is your scent different now? I took her somewhere safe. Why are you here?" I cross my arms over my chest. She doesn't even look down, which either means that she's into girls or she is mated.

"I'm here to find my friend. So where is she? I can smell her on you." As always, she's fiery.

"What do you mean you can smell her on me? What are you?" I growl at her as I take another step in her direction.

"I could ask you the same thing! According to her, you were a human, but as far as I can tell, you're a shifter. Now, tell me where she is! She is in danger with you!" If she is a shifter, too, she should know not to treat me the way she is right now. Her bear will be telling her that she's putting herself in danger.

"I *am* a shifter, but not like you think I am. I'm from the Alaskan islands." Her face goes from fierce to shock in a blink of an eye. So, she *does* know about the bears that live on our islands. The shock is a mere moment before she comes back at me.

"So, you're a Kodiak? If you want to protect Georgie, you need to make sure the tribe you are with doesn't get to her." She places her hands on her hips, shifting her weight to one side. She is definitely a bear. I can see it in her eyes and the way that she holds herself. If I hadn't grown up with my bear tribe, I would have missed her scent telling me she isn't part of a tribe. What worries me is why I haven't picked up her scent sooner.

Well, if you would've allowed the Tribe to summon me before you left, then you might've known a lot of things sooner. We definitely wouldn't have been shot and almost died, my bear gruffs. I'm never going to live this down.

"I know. That's why she is where she is right now. If you want to help me protect her, you need to take her to this cabin and *make* her wait for me there." I gave her the address before going to Dan. "She's in a cave right now. She fainted after my battle with him. Knowing her, she is probably on her way back here."

I glance over my shoulder, and she nods before taking off toward my scent.

I'm sorry, Georgie, but I need more time to find out why they want you.

Turning back to Dan I notice he's reverted to his human form. The deep valleys where my claws dug into him have pierced his heart. I'm going to have to figure out what to say to Garrett and the chief. Otherwise, they will find out I'm not a Grizzly like everyone thinks I am.

Picking him up and placing him over my shoulders, I jog back into the tribe to let Garrett and the chief know that something has happened to him. Hoping that maybe they won't see right through me.

Dawn is approaching as I reach the tribe. The few people still in the clearing stare at me while I head straight to the Chief. Garrett is beside him when I reach them. Dropping Dan at their feet, they finally spot the deep claw marks in his chest.

If you look closely enough, they may be able to see the spine.

"What's the meaning of this? Who did this?" The Chief stands from his seated position and sluggishly comes down to where Dan lies.

"I found him like this. I've never seen marks like this before." In truth, I have, but I want him to tell me if he knows. Because every few years, all the Tribe chiefs meet with my Tribe.

"Garrett, let the patrols know that we have visitors. We need to proceed with caution. You two take this man to the burial grounds." The chief points behind me and then motions for another person to approach him. "Bring this man some shorts."

"Thank you, chief." I smile at the tribe member passing me clothing. "Thank you."

They nod and scamper away. I dress quickly due to the stares from the unmated females. They don't hide the fact that they find me interesting, but they aren't Georgie. No one can ever compare to Georgie.

"Where did you find him? He was supposed to have been patrolling the grounds." the Chief questions me, his eyes flickering between his human and his bear's shades.

"I found him on the patrol trail. I was heading out to bathe when I came across him. That's when I noticed him and the large bear tracks," I answer him. The fact that I don't hesitate astounds me.

The Chief nods as he watches the two men he ordered to take Dan to the burial grounds. As much as I should be upset that he is dead, I'm not. Because if anything, I was in the right to protect my mate from another male. And if he fell, that just meant that he isn't worthy of producing offspring.

Chief Mateo stares over the people who are gathering and holds up his hands to quiet the murmuring. "We need to be on the lookout for a large bear. Make sure the cubs are within your sight. No one is allowed out at night unless with another bear and on patrol. Do not worry, fellow clansmen. We will find out who did this, and they will pay!"

I glance around at the plethora of expressions of the tribe. Some worried, others angry, while others grieving their clansman's loss. The only thing I need to worry about is how I will get to Georgie.

When I reach her at the cabin, if Gracie even takes her there, I know for a fact that she will not allow me to leave. Which put me in an even worse predicament.

But I have to feel her again; I need my lips on hers.

Chapter Six

GEORGINNA

I wake to the crackling of a fire. A makeshift bed lies underneath me. Where the hell am I? I stand and look around. It seems to be a cave. My eyes widen as realization kicks in. That enormous bear who killed the grizzly grabbed me and must've brought me here. But why? Why save me and bring me to his home?

One thing I know for certain is I won't wait and find out. I have to look for the opening. There's a glimmer of light shining on my right. I make my way quickly before it returns. As I get closer, I spot the light from the moon, telling me I'm on the right path.

Once I'm out of the cave, I start through the woods. *He has to be here somewhere.* The sound of leaves being crushed under the weight of someone or something comes from beyond me. I hide behind the nearest tree and wait.

That scent is somewhat familiar, the voice in my head notices. *It's not Langdon, though,* she finishes.

I glance slowly around the tree. Taking a deep breath, I quickly turn back against the tree.

What's she doing here? How did she find me so quickly? I know she couldn't have followed my signal from my phone because it's dead.

"Georgie, I know you're here. Come out. We need to go back. It's too dangerous out here. Please," Gracie says as she gets closer. I roll my eyes and lay back on the tree, looking up at the sky.

You may as well listen to her. She's relentless. Plus, I believe she is that scent we found.

How did she find me, and how did she know I left?

I roll off the tree, facing Gracie. "There you are. We need to get out of here. I saw a bear out there. It's been killed by something big. Let's go back before we're next," she says as she wraps her arm around me.

"How'd you find me? My phone died, so there's no way you could track me?" I question. Her finding me out in these woods is a bit odd. Her lips form a thin line, and she shrugs her shoulders.

"I just got lucky, I guess. You're not as quiet as you think. I just followed you from a distance. I figured I'd let you find out how dangerous it is out here. But I *did* try to get to you before the bear got to you, but he was too fast for me. Then that bigger bear came in, and it scared the living shit out of me. It took you with it, I'm guessing to its cave or something."

There's something she's not telling us, the voice warns.

What do you mean? It sounds like a plausible story. What could she possibly be hiding? It seems as though a part of me doesn't believe her, but I don't see why she would lie.

I follow her out of the woods. "We'll start packing tonight and meet Langdon at a cabin in Big Sky, Montana. I saw him on my way here. He told me to take you there. He doesn't want you to be in danger, saying he has business to take care of, then he will meet us there."

What! He was here. Why didn't he come to me? I need to see him.

I start to turn back. *No. We need to do as he said. We're no good to him dead. He will find us, and then we can spend the rest of our lives together,* the voice stops me. I look to the sky, hoping for some divine intervention to bring us back together *now*. Nothing comes, so I relent and continue back with Gracie.

When we arrive at the cabin, all I want is to be back in Langdon's arms. I can't believe I let Gracie and that stupid voice talk me into coming here. We were so close to him. *I* was so close to him. It's easy for them to say to wait. They don't know how it feels to be apart from the one who completes you.

I guess I better make myself comfortable here. At least I know he knows where to find me; I hope he comes for me soon. I don't know how long I can last apart from him. Standing in the living room, I look around, taking in the spacious cabin. On the far side of the room, a fireplace burns. In front of the fireplace are two brown leather recliners with a table between them.

Bookshelves line the walls on the left-hand side, with a mahogany executive desk in front of them. To my right is more floor-to-ceiling bookshelves with doorways to other rooms.

I think I may like it here.

I walk through one of the doorways, which leads to a kitchen. It's the type of kitchen you would expect in a cabin. A brick oven-style stove is the center of attention, followed by the rock-lined bar-top. All the cabinets are built from the same oak wood that the cabin is made of.

I don't cook, but this kitchen is amazing. I wouldn't mind making something here. Walking back into the living area, I turn through the other door. There's a hallway with four doors, two on each side. Every door is shut except for one, which is cracked open. One of the other doors opens, and Gracie pops her head out, and I jump.

"Geez, Grace. You scared the hell out of me."

She laughs. "Sorry. Charlie and I call this room, okay? We're gonna take a nap, then we can go explore some."

I smile and shake my head. "Enjoy." I wink at her, and she shuts the door.

I continue to the room with the open door, curious to see what's inside. I push the door, and something draws me to a familiar scent. Walking to a set of drawers, I open the top drawer, a Polaroid picture of a little boy with his arm around a bear pokes out. The thing that catches my eye is the emerald-green eyes of the boy. I study the picture and try to see any signs that this could be who I think it is. No, it can't be. Why would a picture of Langdon be here? He said he was from Alaska. Why would anything this sentimental be here? There are a lot of people with eyes that color.

I put the picture back and snoop through the rest of the room, hoping to find some clue that Langdon was here. Most of the drawers are empty, except for a few clothes in one of the bottom ones. Obviously, someone lived here at some point. Nothing has been left, just the picture and some clothes. I walk over to the bed and plop down on my back, staring at the ceiling. I think back to the late nights Lang and I stayed up talking. Did he ever mention a cabin?

I lay in bed, trying to bring my breathing back to normal. Langdon turns toward me, propping his head up with his hand.

"So, you really have never been far outside Oklahoma? Why? Aren't you curious about what's out there?"

A face-splitting smile crosses my lips. I turn to face him, mimicking him. "I've never really had the chance or reason to. I've always worked or gone to school. There was never time. Gracie and I have gone to New Orleans for spring break at Mardi Gras. It was fun, but no, I've always been here. What about you? Have you lived anywhere besides Alaska?"

He kisses me and then joins me on his back. It's his turn to stare at the ceiling. "Yeah, I've traveled. I left Alaska when I was eighteen. I wanted to explore and not be tied down. I traveled through Washington, Oregon, Utah, Montana, and pretty much every state between Alaska and here, and to answer your question, I did live in one place before coming to Oklahoma."

Turning to his side, he grabs the back of my head and kisses me. Suddenly, I forget what we were talking about. His hand travels down as he kisses my neck under my ear. Just the right spot for me to feel it all the way down. He reaches the apex of my thighs.

"All ready for me," he growls as his fingers circle my clit. He pushes two fingers inside me, bringing me closer to the edge. I writhe under his touch. His lips find my mouth once again as he continues the ministrations.

"I want you inside me," I breathe huskily into his mouth. He smiles as his fingers continue their assault. I grip the sheets under me as my climax reaches its tipping point. "Oh God, Langdon," I scream as my orgasm bursts through me. He removes his fingers and kisses me with fervor. I savor every taste of his mouth, holding firmly to the back of his head.

He lifts his head, staring down at me and smiling.

"So, you never really answered my question about where you lived outside of Alaska," I say, smirking, My fingers comb through his tousled hair. Damn, he

is so sexy. He kisses me and then lays beside me. "I've a cabin in Big Sky, Montana. I bought it when I was 18 after I left home. I needed somewhere to myself, where I can always go back to besides Alaska."

I lay my head on his chest as I fall asleep...

"That's why this place is so familiar." I sit up on the bed. So that *was* Langdon in that picture. This must be his room.

That's a good reason to stay here, the voice chimes in.

It definitely is! A sense of calm fills me, knowing that this cabin is his home away from home. I crawl under the covers, and the scent of sandalwood, cinnamon and Langdon hits my senses. I bring the blanket to my face, reveling in the calming familiarity of it. Laying down, I cuddle his blanket.

"...I know, but I'm not going to wake her up. It's been a long, exhausting trip for her, and she needs the rest." I open my eyes and look toward the door. It's cracked, but Gracie is standing out there.

She can't whisper to save her life, the voice says. I roll my eyes.

Hey, at least her heart's in the right place. She's trying; leave her alone. A chuckle escapes me, and I shake my head. I stretch my legs off the bed and glance at my phone. Damn. It's already nine in the morning. I slept for fifteen hours, how is that possible?

Jumping up, I head for the door. As soon as I open it, Gracie startles. "Shit!" She puts a hand over her heart. "You scared the shit out of me. I thought you were asleep."

"Good morning to you, too." I laugh. "You're not very good at whispering, by the way. You should've woken me up sooner. I didn't realize I slept for fifteen hours."

She smiles her half-smile and shrugs. "You haven't had much sleep lately. I figured you could use every bit you get."

I wrap her in a hug. She's always been there for me, no matter what. I don't know what I'd do without her. She holds me at arm's length.

"Are you ready to explore what Big Sky has to offer?" I answer with a smile and a nod.

"Georgie, slow down. We need to rest." I look back at Charlie hunched over, trying to catch his breath. Gracie stands beside him, rubbing his back for support. Like me, she doesn't seem to be fazed by the amount of climbing we have done. We've been hiking on Cascade Lake Trail. It's a one-thousand-four-hundred-foot elevation, and we've done about five hundred feet so far.

The only reason we have to stop every ten feet or so is for Charlie. You would think out of the three of us, he would be the most fit and have more stamina, but he doesn't. I sit on the stump of a fallen tree and grab a snack out of my bag. "I guess we could use a snack break." I look around at the magnificent surroundings. Wildflowers mixed with tall pine trees as well as birds chirping in the distance.

"You know, there's a waterfall not too far from here. We should go check it out," I say, standing and pointing to the right. I can hear the flow of the water, and it sounds like it's less than a mile away.

Something draws my attention halfway down the path we just climbed.

Someone's close, the voice in my head says as I head down the path. Why does this always happen? Why am I drawn to things that could get me in trouble? Of course, on the other hand, it seems to always lead me to Langdon. Maybe that's how it is now. The possibility of Langdon being here urges me to move faster until I come to a screeching halt. Wait, that feeling isn't Langdon.

It's something else. I look around and start toward the feeling. I need to find out what that is. If it's not Langdon, I need to know.

The feeling becomes stronger until I reach the source. Confused, I look around.

Nothing.

What the hell?

I sense *something* here, yet I'm standing in the middle of a clearing in the woods. Looking around, I try to find the source but no one's here. I head back the way I came, toward Gracie and Charlie.

"Hey, where'd you go?" Gracie says as I walk up to them.

"I thought I heard something, so I went to check it out. It turns out it was nothing. I guess I'm going crazy." I laugh. "Let's go back to the cabin. It's getting late, and you both can rest." They both nod.

"That's a great idea," Gracie says as we turn back the way we came.

I walk through the front door and head toward the kitchen. I realized I hadn't eaten much today, and I'm starving. It's already seven o'clock.

"I'm going to make something to eat. Do you guys want anything?" I ask as Gracie and Charlie enter the living room.

"Not for me," Charlie says as he walks past us. "I'm in desperate need of a shower. Goodnight."

"Night, Charlie," I call out to him as he disappears down the hall.

Gracie walks into the kitchen and opens the fridge. "Lucky for us, the food here is still good. There's no telling how long this stuff has been here," She says, taking out a pack of luncheon meat.

I lean on the island in the middle of the kitchen, crossing my arms across my waist. "Did you know this was Langdon's cabin?"

She pauses, turning to look at me. A guilty look crosses her face. My eyes widen.

"You *did* know, didn't you?!" I can't believe this.

"I'm sorry, Gina. He said it was his cabin when he moved here from Alaska. He thought this would be the best place for you to be. I didn't mean to keep secrets from you. I didn't think it would matter if he knew where to find us."

She *does* have a point. I don't mind at all that this is his cabin. In fact, I'm glad. It gives me a chance to look around and learn more about him. I know surprisingly little of the man, yet we've gotten so close. I don't know what draws me to him; I've never felt anything like it.

"Don't worry about it. Now that I know, I can do some snooping," I tell her, and we both laugh. It feels good to laugh again. It's been so long. Since I thought Lang died, nothing around me made me feel cheerful. I still feel lost, but knowing he's alive and coming back to me gives me something to look forward to.

After Gracie goes to bed, I embark on my new mission; to learn more about Langdon Kenai. The first place I start is the executive desk. There's got to be something here. Pulling the top left drawer open, I see a stack of papers. Maybe there's something in here that will tell me a little bit. The top few papers are just a bunch of numbers I'm not going to even try to understand. I get further down the stack, and one in particular catches my eye. It seems to be a letter.

My dear, sweet boy,

I know life hasn't always gone according to plan, but I want you to remember where you came from. Enclosed, you will find a picture. Remember, no matter what, I will always be with you in spirit, no matter where you may roam.

Love, Mom.

I put the rest of the papers on the desk and stare at the letter from his mother. Why would a picture of him and a bear remind him of her? Were they around bears as a family? This just brings more questions than answers.

Placing the letter on top of the pile, I put the whole thing back in the drawer. What happened in Alaska to make him leave? I search the rest of his desk and turn up empty-handed.

Well, that didn't go according to plan.

I walk into Lang's bedroom and continue my mission. I search until exhaustion strikes. The only personal items I find are the letter and picture. I guess I'll have to go to the source, Langdon, to find the answers.

I crawl into bed and settle in.

Don't worry, you find out all you need to know when the time comes, the voice chimes in. Oh great, she's awake.

I roll my eyes. *Thanks, that's so much help.* She's no help at all.

You're welcome. Now, get some rest so we can get through what tomorrow brings. With that, my eyes drift as sleep claims me.

Chapter Seven

LANGDON

"Langdon!"

Turning, I spot Garrett running up to me as I make my way back to my tent. We are the last tribe to leave, and I'm not about to go when everyone wants to know how and who killed Dan. As long as they don't think it was me I will be fine. But the moment I become the suspect, I will need to be very careful.

"What's up, Garrett?" I stand to let him catch up to me. This whole Bear Meeting is starting to get under my skin. I'm ready to get out of here and see Georgie.

"Chief Mateo would like us to scour the land to see if we can find any evidence of this massive bear," Garrett answers me as I watch him glance over his shoulder.

"Sure, Garrett. When do we leave?" My thoughts begin to swirl around in my head to figure out how I'm going to keep Garrett from following Gracie's scent. This way, it won't lead him to the cave and find Georgie's scent there.

"We're leaving now. Go grab some stuff to take with you. We'll be gone for a few days."

Georgie isn't going to like that, my bear comments.

Fuck don't I know it.

Garrett and I head toward the spot where Dan was killed. There is no telling what he is going to find there. I just hope that the bear goddess Artio will be on my side and let me keep Garrett away from Georgie.

"I can't seem to pick up a scent. There's a scent here that I haven't smelled before." Garrett kneels, running his hand over the blood-stained grass.

"It's probably the bear that killed him." I begin to worry that he is going to head off to the cave and in turn find Georgie and Gracie's scent.

"You know, sometimes I think it would have been easier to have allowed you to die? Because you are not as smart as I thought you'd have been." Garrett glances up at me as I stand, waiting to leave.

"Yeah, well everyone needs a lacky right?" I ask, shrugging. He glares back at me. He knows I was talking about him and Chief Mateo.

"I'll pretend I didn't hear that." Garrett rises and brushes off his pants. I follow him south, away from the cave where I hid Georgie.

While we continue down the territory line, the memory of the time I overheard Chief Mateo and Garrett talking about Georgie and her family prickles...

The night is cool as I carry my tent over to a secluded spot. As I pass the Chief's tent, I recognize Garrett's voice coming from the makeshift home.

"Chief, the last survivor was at that bar. She looks just like her mother. I couldn't believe she was there. After all those years thinking that everyone was gone, and then she shows up here in our territory!" The mention of Georgie gets me thinking. What were they talking about? Georgie is human, what do they want with her?

"I knew those Rowan's had her hidden away. But there was no Rowan name in the school system," the chief's voice floats out from the tent flaps. This blows my mind. Are they talking about THE Rowans? The ones that were demolished back when I was just a cub? I never knew that they had a cub, at least my parents never told me they did.

"They must have changed her name. Because I KNOW that girl was a Rowan," Garrett answers him, his shadow's arms flying around.

I have never been around the Rowan tribe, but I had heard the stories of them being slaughtered in the middle of the night. Could this grizzly tribe be the ones to do it? It had been a massacre from what we had been taught. The teachers wouldn't even let us see the pictures.

"That would be the only way to hide her. We need to find her again. Otherwise, it could cause an uprising, and we don't need that," Chief Mateo answers him while he sat in a chair. The smell of the kinnikinnick coming from the tent. It always makes my stomach turn.

Coming out of my memory of that night, I glance over to Garrett. Would he answer my question if I ask him? Probably not, but hell what can it hurt?

"So, out of curiosity. Why were you after the human girl?" Garrett turns to me and glares before he continues to walk away. He isn't one to say anything. Hell, he probably doesn't know why his chief—and I say *his* because I'm not a Grizzly even if I have to act like it—wants Georgie dead.

But then again, he may know. That's why I need to figure out all that he knows.

"She's not human and are you sad that your lover is gone?" he asks while he sniffs at a tree.

As much as it would be weird to a human, it isn't to me. But he doesn't know that he summoned my bear that day. And he doesn't know that I now know that my father's friends were slaughtered. I just have to figure out a way to get this information to my father. Maybe I can get Gracie to take Georgie to my birth tribe. It would be safer for her there with the strongest bears in the world. I only hope that my father will take them both in.

Hopefully, he will come and help us. I know that he will be very upset that another bear other than our Elder awoke my bear, but that doesn't mean that I'm not as strong as my other tribe-mates.

"I had just met her a couple of months before the night you attacked me. She was clinging to me, so why not? Plus, she gave it up the first night that we met." I shrug, he doesn't need to know that I had known her longer. I hate that I've made her out to be a slut, but I need him to think that she doesn't mean much to me.

So that when I leave for the cabin he won't come snooping. Because I need to tell her about me. She needs to know about herself. I hate that I will have to be the one to tell her.

Hell, if she is a bear— and a Kodiak at that. Why doesn't Gracie tell Georgie? And I know for certain that Gracie is a bear. So, why if they are both bears has Gracie kept that from Georgie? Is Gracie in on keeping her away from the people who killed their tribe?

There are so many more questions now that I know she is from the tribe that was wiped off the face of the Earth. But I still don't know why they had attacked her tribe. What did they gain from removing one of the Kodiak tribes from the Earth?

"Yeah, well you seem like you aren't interested in the females that are in our tribe. Are you sure she didn't mean anything?" The sneer that graces his face gets under my skin. He needs to back the fuck up.

"I'll answer your question when you let me ask mine." I walk past him into the river. The wind is already carrying her scent away from this part of the forest.

"The questions that you're asking are not ones I can give you answers to. Maybe one day you will be able to learn them. But right now, they won't be answered."

I shake my head and continue on. We stop searching for the night around midnight, which is when I made my exit. I still have to come back, so I leave my tent where it is and slip into the darkness of the tree line.

Shifting to my bear when I'm far enough away from the territory line makes the journey a lot faster as I head to Georgie. When I get to the cabin, the sun is just starting to rise behind the mountains on the right side of the wooden hut.

I slow at the edge of the forest line. It wouldn't be good if I show up in my bear form. In my haste to get to her. I have forgotten to grab some extra clothes. That's what happens for letting my emotions get in my way of things.

My eyes search the area, trying to think of a way to get into the cabin. The flora and fauna I had planted earlier in the year are dying due to the lack of water. I know that she has her girlfriend here, but what surprises me is that there is a male with them. He is human, so it would probably freak him out if he saw a big-ass bear roaming through the inside of the cabin. Along with Georgie since I'm sure she isn't aware that she is a bear.

I made my way around to the side where my window is and shift back to my human form. The breeze caresses my skin as I move to the window. I haven't ever snuck into my own home before, but it's sort of exciting. My only hope is that she hasn't locked it because then it will be a bitch getting in. Luck is on my side, and I slide the window open, allowing a cool breeze into the room.

Damn I really needed to visit this place more often, I think to myself as I enter the room. You can tell by the scent of the room that it hadn't been inhabited for a long time. But then I can smell her scent, which is slowly taking over the other. I could only hope that she will stay here until I can ensure she is safe.

I glance over to the bed, and there she is. Cuddled in on herself under the covers. It's a good thing that I have clothes stored here. But that isn't what I've come for. I gently close the window and then head over to the bed. It excites me to see her here, knowing that she has chosen this one over the others. Standing here watching her sleep is my new favorite pastime.

She hadn't changed in the year that we had been apart. My heart soars as she moans my name in her sleep. Georgie has always been a wonderful person and an even more beautiful soul. The Goddess Artio blessed me with the best mate I could ever have dreamed of.

I know now why I haven't really been into any of the females in my birth tribe. They don't have the qualities that the woman in my bed has. She turns to face the door, and I make my way over to the bed. She has washed the bedding, but it still holds some of my scent.

Now though, it is immersed in hers. The glint of light reflects off something on the bedside table. I go over to it and realize that she had taken out the picture of my mother and me when I was cub. How I miss that woman, but I decided what I wanted to do with my life and I'm so glad that I did.

Replacing the picture, I pull back the covers. Georgie shivers at the cold until I pull her close to me. She melts into me and sighs in her sleep. I haven't felt this relaxed since I was shot and ripped from her side.

I snuggle into her and tug the comforter back up around me. She's wearing one of my shirts. My scent mixing with hers just like it will when I convince her to do a bonding ceremony. I allow my breathing to regulate and finally fall into a deep and relaxing sleep.

Chapter Eight

GEORGINNA

As I wake up and stretch my limbs, someone is beside me. I'm almost too afraid to look, but a part of me already knows who it is. I slowly turn my head, and a flood of emotions rush into my body.

Langdon lies beside me in all his glory. I'm tempted to jump on top of him and show him how much I've missed him, but instead, I turn to my side, rest my head on my hand and watch him. I can't believe he's here. He *is here*, right?

He sure is. I can feel it with certainty, the voice says in all her giddiness. I can't say I blame her.

Look over his upper body above the blanket; *is he naked?* I lift the sheets slightly, not wanting to wake him just yet, and sure enough, he is. I lick my lips.

I move closer to him and kiss him. His eyes slowly open. "Hey beautiful," he says with a smile so sexy it takes all I have not to climb him right here right now. I grab hold of him, never wanting to let go. I want to say something, but not a damn word comes out. I just cuddle close to him and take in his scent. "I missed you too, Georgie."

Oh, sweet Lord. I missed hearing my name on his lips. I look up at him, and he cups my head, kissing me passionately. Lifting the covers, I straddle him, needing to be closer to him. He grabs my ass as he deepens the kiss. His hands slide up my shirt, his touch igniting my back.

"Mmm," I moan into his mouth, savoring every taste of him as if it is my last. I start grinding my hips on top of him and feel him harden beneath me.

"I missed how you feel on top of me," he says huskily against the corner of my mouth. I answer with mewls of pleasure. He lifts me long enough to pull my panties off, and I slowly sit on him, his cock sliding inside me.

Oh, my fuck, I miss how he feels. I start moving, but he stops me. I feel him twitch, and he looks up at me with a smirk. Then he picks me up, slamming me down on top of him. "Fuck!" That feels so damn good. He starts kissing my neck under my ear as I move on top of him.

He moves so fast, and suddenly, I'm under him. He grabs my wrists and holds them above my head, pinning them down so I can't move.

"Thank Artio, we found each other again." He starts to kiss me, starting from my lips, then moves south, pulling out of me. His lips trace a trail down my body, taking his time. My body arches as his mouth invades my nipples, sucking and biting one as he caresses the other. The voice inside my head starts to roar inside me. A sound I've never heard before. A sound filled with the same emotions and pleasure I feel.

He continues his kisses south, his hand still caressing my breast. Before he reaches the apex of my thighs, he hovers his mouth over my clit. So close yet so far away. I try desperately to bring my hips closer, but he holds me down with his free hand.

"Not yet," he says as a devious look appears, telling me what he's planning.

He blows his hot breath on my clit, and a shudder moves through my body. He releases my hands and lifts my hips to his mouth, devouring me. "Oh God, I forgot how sweet you taste," he moans as he brings me to the edge of the abyss. My body riding high, and I feel my orgasm coming, edging closer and closer. "Come for me, beautiful." His words do me in, and I explode. He kisses my bud and lays beside me, his head resting on his hand. I lie the same way, facing him.

"I can't believe you're really here. How long will you be staying?" I dread his answer, because I know deep down he has to go back so they don't come looking for him.

"I'm staying for a couple of days then I have to go back. They don't know I left, plus there's still more information I need to gather." That's what I was afraid of. "I guess we'll just have to make the most of our time together." He smiles as he leans in, pulling me into a kiss.

Chapter Nine

GEORGINNA

As I walk into the kitchen, I hear Langdon and Gracie. "I'm glad you were able to make it. Georginna's been going a little crazy without you around." I walk in and find them in the kitchen.

"Thanks, Grace. I appreciate that," I say with a smirk. "Well, it's true, isn't it? Now you can relax for a couple of days," she says, gesturing toward Lang. Walking up to him, I wrap my arms around him. The top of my head comes to his chin. He kisses the crown of my head and encircles his arms around me.

I look up at him. "While I have you here, I have some questions for you."

He answers with a sexy-as-hell smile. "Ask me anything. I have nothing to hide from you." I look over to Gracie, and she nods, giving me a knowing smile. Taking him by the hand, I lead him to the living room. I take the picture of him and a bear out of my pocket and hand it to him, then I walk to the desk, taking the note out of the drawer. "Done some snooping, have you?" he says with a smirk.

"A little. I want to get to know you more. I also had time to kill while I was waiting for you." I sit next to him on the couch. "The first question I have is, what significance does this bear have to you? Your mom mentions it in her letter. I'm guessing she was bidding you farewell when you left home, but I need to know."

Nerves wrack my body. Not knowing much about him scares me. I love him with everything I am, yet I don't know a single thing, only that he's from Alaska.

He sits back on the couch, laying his arm behind me, turns toward me, and takes my hand in his, bringing it to his lips. "That bear was a part of my family in a way. We grew up in a village surrounded by bears and wildlife. We coincided with the bears there. That particular bear came around very often, and my mother wanted to capture the moment."

Bears and people getting along with each other? I've never heard of that before. But of course, I've never been to Alaska either, so it's not impossible.

"Speaking of Alaska," I say, scooting closer to him, needing more of his touch. "What happened to make you leave?" I know he told me he needed a change of scenery when we met, but after reading the note, I need to know more.

He gives me a look that tells me he doesn't want to tell me everything. *Why?* Did something bad happen that he's afraid will get out? Is that the reason why they took him? The longer his silence is, the more questions race through my mind. He runs his hand along my jawline.

"My family wanted me to live up to the traditions of my ancestors, but I just wanted to live my life the way I planned to without answering to others. I wanted to be free. I felt the only way to do that was to get as far away as possible. And I did," he says simply with a shrug.

I look into his eyes, and I can tell he's telling me the truth, or at least as much as he's willing to tell. A part of me feels he's holding back. But of course, we have the rest of our lives to delve deeper. I cuddle into him, I missed the way he feels next to me. I could stay in his arms forever.

After spending the whole day together, walking the trails, and enjoying ourselves in the bedroom. I decide to take some time rummaging through the books he's collected. Lang has gone outside and gather firewood. He noticed we were running low, and the air was starting to cool. Running my fingers along the spines, I realize how old these books are. They are the kind you find in ancient libraries or lining the shelves of the expensive homes in Europe in the early 1800s.

I make it to the end of the bookshelf and walk toward the window to my left. Peeling back the curtain, I find Langdon talking to Gracie. They seem to be in a heated discussion. They look out into the woods, and suddenly, their stances change.

What happens next will haunt me for the rest of my days. All of a sudden, both of them start to shift into something I thought was only in stories and fairytales. Langdon grows taller, hair covering his huge, bulky body. Gracie, not as big, grows to double her height. Hair covers her body as well. Snouts and gnarling teeth take the place of their nose and mouth. Hands and feet transform into huge paws. A few minutes pass by, and I stare at the huge Kodiak bears where my love and best friend once stood.

Why I know what kind of bears they are is beyond me. I've never really studied wildlife, let alone species of bears. They start running into the woods. I stand here, frozen in shock. I thought Langdon had secrets, but nothing like this!

"I can't believe it!" I whisper, staring at Langdon and Gracie as they run into the woods, toward whatever sound caught their attention. Why didn't they tell me? Why keep that from me? Sure, I would've freaked. I mean, who wouldn't? But they didn't even give me a chance. *I need to sit down.*

I walk to the couch and plop down, laying my head on the back and staring at the ceiling. What am I going to do? I will *never* be able to look at them the same again. How could I? How long have they been keeping this from me? I thought I knew Gracie better than that. *How could she?*

I close my eyes and take deep, calming breaths to steady my nerves. They'll be back, and I don't have one earthly idea what I'm going to do. How do I handle this?

It's so crazy how the last year has been. First, I lose the love of my life. Then I find out that not only is he alive, but he also happens to be a bear shifter?

Oh, and also, I have this voice in my head from an entity separate from myself, apparently. How am I supposed to come to terms with something like this?

Rising from the bed, I make my way to the living room. I need to see if there's any information that could explain what Langdon and Gracie are. Is Charlie the same?

As I reach the bookshelf, a sound from the other room captures my attention. With each step I take, my anxiety spikes higher and higher. "Charlie?" I call, hoping it's just him.

I turn into the kitchen and see dishes on the floor. "Charlie, what are you doing?" I question. He must've dropped the dishes and gone to get towels to clean it up. I bend down to pick them up and immediately drop them, seeing Charlie lying on the ground, blood pooling under his head. "Holy hell! Charlie?" I call to him. I reach for Charlie, but before I can get closer, someone grabs me from behind.

"Let me go!" I yell and kick my leg back, catching him in the groin. I run toward the door, making my way around the furniture. I need to find Langdon and Gracie.

I hear the furniture scraping against the floor and things crashing.

"What the hell?" When I look back, I see a familiar face before everything goes black.

Chapter Ten

LANGDON

Having noticed that our firewood is getting low and that the weather is cooling off, I have been in the woods to find replenishments. When I get back to the cabin, Gracie marches up to me, her expression telling me she isn't in a good mood.

"What do you think you're doing? You said that you are leaving in a couple of days and the only thing that you give Georgie is that half-truth!" Gracie's finger presses against my chest, and my bear isn't too happy with her disrespect.

"I couldn't very well just come out and tell her what I am. That would tell her about you, too. So, have you told her what you and she are? You've been with her a whole lot longer than I have and you haven't told her anything." I don't like her blaming me for not telling Georgie the whole truth.

"I've noticed that she is starting to act differently. Since she met you, her bear has come to the surface. That's the only way that she could have known that you were where she found you that day." Gracie crosses her arms as she cocks her hips to the side. If I didn't know any better, I'm sure Gracie is a ranked female.

"Well, if that's true, then she's closer to shifting. If she shifts and doesn't know she is going to, she's going to freak out. Why would you not tell her when she was younger?" I drop the firewood and step up to her when something catches my attention.

Gracie's gaze snaps in the direction that I am staring in. I can't quite figure out what it was until I recognize the scent from one of the other Grizzlies that I have patrolled with. This isn't going to

HAUNTED LOVE

be good. I turn to Gracie and nod to her, and she nods back.

Shifting with Gracie is a little weird as I have been keeping my bear side away from the Grizzlies to hide my actual tribe, the Kodiak tribe. The only way that they would know that I came here is if I hadn't covered my tracks well enough. Which means that I have led them straight to Georgie.

I'm going to have to fix this quickly. They can't find her. If they do, I don't know what they will do with her. I haven't found out why they are trying to get rid of her and why they destroyed the Rowan tribe.

Gracie and I run through the forest toward the bears who are barreling through the brush. If anything, I need to get these bears away from Georgie. I have to protect her and figure out why these people killed her tribe.

Reaching the first bear, I pounce into him, creating a domino effect on the others behind him. I stand on my hind legs locking into battle with one as Gracie takes on another. I haven't been as good of a fighter in my bear form since I left my tribe without letting them unlock my bear. But

I'm bigger, and I'm not going to let them get to Georgie.

I swipe my massive paw across the next bear's face, sending him into a tree not too far from us while taking out another. Gracie is doing pretty well for herself as she sinks her fangs into a bear's front leg. I need to make a mental note to never be on the wrong side of her. Bigger or not, I won't lose life or limb to the bear fighting beside me.

When they start to turn tail and run, I can't understand why. They out match us two to one, and then it hits me. It has to be a diversion. Garrett must have set this up to get us away from Georgie, and I fell for it. That also means that he knows that I'm protecting her and that I have known where she is this whole time.

Fuck me! How could I be so stupid to let this happen. I turn and run back to the cabin. Gracie on my heels as we burst from the underbrush of the woods. I can clearly make out his scent as we get closer. Shifting back to my human form, I run into the house.

Couches are overturned, and lamps are broken on the floor. Georgie must have put up a hell of a fight, but in the end, he seems to have gotten the better of her. I don't know what to do. Gracie comes in, spots all the disarray, and falls to her knees. We are going to have to find her. If not, I don't know how long they are going to keep her alive.

Gracie rises from her position on the floor and begins to search the cabin. I forgot that Charlie was still here and run behind her until I see her crouched on the floor with him. She holds him in her arms, rocking him. Charlie is breathing, and the pace of his heartbeat are normal. I go up to them and kneel at Gracie's level.

"He's going to be fine. I'll be right back, I need to get some clothes and then I'll help you take him to the back bedroom."

Gracie glances up at me and nods as she holds him and rocks. If I had found Georgie this way, I'm sure that I would be the same with her. Jogging to my room, I grab some clothes and then make my way back to the kitchen where Charlie is coming to.

Taking one of his arms and wrapping it around my neck, we take him to the bedroom and lay him on the mattress. Gracie runs and grabs some ice to place on his head. A huge knot is rising from where he must have been hit over the head with something. Charlie is lucky that he isn't bleeding out.

"We have to figure out how to get Georgie back. But what do you want to do with Charlie?" I question Gracie as she returns to us, fully clothed.

Charlie goes in and out of consciousness as Gracie places the ice on his head. I wouldn't worry as much if the man was a shifter. But since he is just a human, I don't like the fact of possibly leaving him here at the house alone.

"He will be fine. His pupils are dilating, and he's breathing." Gracie glances back at me and holds the ice on his head. "The other problem is that we now need to get Georgie. Do you know who it was that had taken her?"

"Yeah, it's the tribe that I have been with since I was shot. For some reason, they are dead set on wanting to eliminate Georgie." I pace the bedroom, wracking my brain to figure out how to get word to my father and get his help. "I need you to get a message out to my father. Can you send him a telegram? And then we can meet at the cave I had Georgie at. We need to get more bears to get her back."

"Sure, but I'm not sure if they will make it in time." Gracie stands and takes the towel to the bathroom.

"My family has a plane. We need about fifteen more. They are smaller than us, and we can make that work. Most of them will be gone by the time we return because the Bear Festival is almost over," I explain. Even though I have been gone for so long, I know that I can trust my dad to send help. Especially since I had found my fated mate. The only thing that I need to figure out is why this tribe of Grizzlies killed Georgie's tribe.

"Gracie, do you know why you and Georgie are the only ones alive out of your tribe?" I ask her as she comes back into the room.

"Yeah, but that will be a story for the both of you. I'm sure that Georgie is going to want to know since she was just kidnapped by bears. Then, when we try to rescue her, she is going to freak." Charlie lies on the bed, breathing normally as Gracie covers him up. She then begins to write him a note.

I don't think I would ever be able to go through what she does with being with a human and never being able to tell him what she is. I have never seen bears mated with humans, but that doesn't mean that it doesn't happen. Gracie looks as if she loves him, but what do I know? I didn't even realize that I had found my mate until I lost her, and she found me a year later.

"Well, let's go. Do you know where there is a place that will let me or will have a telegram? I mean why don't they have phones?" Gracie grabs a bag and fills it with clothes.

I'm just going to carry my shorts with me. Carrying bags makes me feel even more cumbersome than I already am. Being a bigger bear doesn't help that matter either.

"The next city still has a telegram. Tell the store owner, Tony, that I sent you. He will send it to my tribe for free. Since he is from my tribe as well. Oh! And don't stare at his scar. He hates that." Gracie nods and kisses Charlie on the forehead before we head out of the cabin.

I pull off my shorts and then shift. Gracie nods to me again and then takes off at a sprint to the town. Turning my huge head to the woods, I go to the cave to find out how fast it has taken them to get Georgie to the tribe.

All I know is that I am going to kill Garrett for taking her. When I get my claws on Mateo for taking my mate's family away from her, he will wish he had never destroyed her tribe.

They don't know what they have brought on themselves by taking my mate away from me.

Chapter Eleven

GEORGINNA

When I open my eyes, everything is still dark. I try to move, but I'm restrained by chains. *What the hell?!* I scoot back to find walls beside and behind me. The feel of rocks covering the walls. I must be in the corner of a cave. Tiny rocks and rough loose earth underneath where I sit.

We're stuck for now, the voice in my head states the obvious.

I roll my eyes. "Of course we're stuck, duh. We're chained up, crouched on the ground."

Sometimes, I think the voice is just the crazy side of me that wants to bring me deeper into craziness.

I try to bring my arms up, but something stops my arms from moving. Cuffs are attached to both of my arms, the metal like a thick bracelet hugging my wrists. I follow a thick chain flowing down and find that it's attached to the shackles at my ankles. Looking around, I need to find a way out. Why would they have me chained down like some sort of animal?

There's no use struggling. I lay my head back against the wall.

Why am I here? What do they want from me?

"You're awake!"

No fucking way! It can't be. I recognize that voice. Slowly, I open my eyes and look at the man who took my world from me and caused all this shit. Rage fills my insides, and all I want to do is kill him.

"Oh good, you recognize me. Well, that's out of the way—"

"What do you want with me?" I interrupt through gritted teeth. I can't believe he found me. I don't even know him, yet he's got an obsession with me.

He steps forward, crouching down, elbows on his knees. "Sweet innocent Georginna Rowan, you don't even realize what you are, do you?" he says with a sadistic grin plastered to his ugly, scarred face. *Rowan?*

"You're mistaken. You have the wrong person. My name is Georginna Mendoza, not Rowan." He stands and straightens, leaning his shoulder against the wall and crossing his arms.

"No, I believe you are the one who's mistaken here. I *know* who you are, but apparently you do not. I was told we got rid of you Rowans, but I guess not. You've been hidden from us for far too long."

"I don't understand. I'm not a Rowan. My parents died when I was thirteen. They were killed in a freak accident in Hobart, Oklahoma. Their name, along with my family's, was Mendoza. I have no idea where you're getting Rowan from." He pushes himself off the wall and gets in my face in an instant.

"Listen here, you little bitch," he says, grabbing my face tight, squishing my cheeks. "I don't like to be called a liar. I know full well who you *really* are. I'm not going to sit here and argue about it. You'll find out when I am good and ready to tell you what you are and why you're here."

Rage fills me, and something thrashes inside me, bubbling to the surface. The scar running from his hairline to his jaw pulsing. He lets go of my face and storms out without another word.

I have to figure out a way out of this. Struggling in these chains won't do a damn thing for me. Bringing my knees to my chest, I tuck in on myself and pray to whoever is listening that I somehow make it out alive.

What am I going to do? How can I trust Langdon and Gracie again? They lied to me. Langdon, I can forgive because we haven't known each other for too long, but Gracie? I don't think I can ever forgive her. She's kept a HUGE secret from me for all these years.

In time, you will understand. She did it for your safety and mine, the voice in my head chimes in.

You keep saying that. Now, that man has said that same thing. What is it that I will 'find out'? It's infuriating. I feel her roll her eyes and settle somewhere inside me. I guess I'll have to be patient, no matter how it annoys me.

My eyes drift and I lay my head on the cold hard ground.

I wake to the sound of footsteps. I straighten up as best as I can, steeling myself for whatever he has in store for me. "Oh good, you're awake," a female voice greets me. I look up and notice a woman in a plaid, dark purple shirt and jeans walking toward me, carrying a tray.

"I'm sorry, Garrett can be a bit of a pain in the ass. He doesn't know how to treat guests."

Seriously? She thinks I'm a guest here? What kind of guest is left chained up?

This woman must be out of her mind.

She looks like the type we can befriend so we can make our escape, the voice says. That's a good idea. I can try to appeal to her humanity and bide my time until I can get back to Langdon.

She sets the tray down beside me and reaches for me. I try to back up. There's no telling what she has planned.

"Easy, it's okay. I just brought you something to eat. It's been nearly a full twenty-four hours since you've been here. I thought you'd be hungry." She raises her hands in surrender. "I'm just going to undo the chains from your wrist so you can eat. Please don't make me regret this. You seem like a nice enough woman. I don't want to have to do something we'll both regret."

I nod in response. Smiling in return, she undoes the chain, and it falls to the ground at my feet.

"Thank you," I grind out, my voice a little hoarse. Placing the tray in front of me, I smell the pleasant aroma of fried venison, potatoes, and corn, which makes my mouth water.

After eating what I can only describe as the best meal I've eaten in a very long time, I feel like I can sleep forever. It surprises me. I've never had venison before, but it was delicious. I'm more of a steak and chicken kind of girl, but I think I will add this as a favorite.

"What's your name?" I ask as she places the cuffs back on my wrists. She reaches behind her and produces a pillow and a small child-size blanket.

"I'm Clara. It's nice to meet you, although I'm sorry it couldn't be under better circumstances," she says as she picks up the now empty tray and heads out. I lay my head on the pillow beside me, my eyes feeling heavier by the second, and bring my legs up to my chest.

A sharp pain strikes my back. I scramble to sit up. "Wake up. It's time to take you to see the doctor." Garrett dips down, unhooking the chain from the cave wall, leaving my hands and feet shackled. "Stand up," he demands, pulling on the chain.

"How am I supposed to move with my feet chained up?" I ask incredulously. I don't see why he has to be such a jackass. He should've sent Clara for me. At least she was more hospitable.

He rolls his eyes and loosens the chains attached to my ankles. "There, that should make it easier. Now let's go." He grabs the chain and we head out of the cave.

When we get outside, I look around. An unfamiliar side of the forest surrounds me. I do my best to put one foot in front of the other, but I fail miserably.

"You know, if you removed the shackles from my ankles, I'd be able to walk better," I say after he pulls on the chain for the umpteenth time. He stops suddenly, and I almost bump into him.

"It's the only way I can assure that you will not try to run."

I look at him incredulously, shaking my head. "How am I supposed to run when you have a hold of the chain?" I say lifting my hands, and the chain pulls his.

He huffs and looks up at the sky. "Fine, I'll remove them from your feet only." Pointing one finger toward me, so close I can smell a musty, pungent aroma emanating from him. "If you make one move to try to escape, I will kill you where you stand."

I lift my hands as best as I can in surrender. "I won't."

He bends and unfastens the chain. I sigh in relief and roll my ankles, feeling the soreness subside. "Thank you."

He stands and hands me the ankle restraints. "Hold these," Are his only words before we resume walking.

"Why do I need to see the doctor? If you're just going to kill me, isn't that redundant?" I don't see why he needs to take me to the doctor. Unless he has other plans for me. I groan and shiver at the thought of him having any kind of ulterior motives.

"There's some blood test that needs to be run. The chief demanded we establish you are who we know you to be before moving forward."

Chief? What kind of cult is this? Oh God, I hope they aren't wanting me to be a participant of some sort of twisted shit. I'd rather die.

We walk up to a small log cabin with a wooden door at the front. A sign hangs over it reading, "Healer." That must be the doctor's office. I glance around, and house-shaped tents surround the area.

Garrett stops at the door and turns to me. "Here's what you're going to do. You will keep your trap shut and do as the doctor says. You *will* behave yourself, or there will be consequences."

I shut my mouth in a tight line and nod, keeping the rolling anger at bay. He nods in return as we enter the cabin.

"Welcome, Georginna. It's nice to see you again." Clara walks my way, wearing a white coat with a stethoscope around her neck. Words escape me. I stand there, unable to speak. The generous woman who cared for me at the cave turns out to be the doctor of this 'cult'? I smile in return.

Around the room, monitors are set up, and a single bed, the kind you would see in a normal doctor's office, with the head of it slightly elevated and rolling wheels underneath, sits in the middle of the room. Clara waves me over. "Sit on the bed, and we can get started."

Garret starts for the door. "Let me know when you're done here," he says to Clara, then walks out.

She rolls up her sleeves and places a small metal tray on a stand beside the bed. "Okay, let's start by taking some blood."

"Why am I here? He wouldn't tell me much. Is this a cult or something? He said the Chief wanted me to get tested. Is this some kind of initiation thing or something?"

She laughs and shakes her head. "No, my dear. We are most definitely not a cult. We are a tribe. We live in groups to hunt and care for each other. As far as why you're here specifically, I'm afraid I cannot tell you. I have been threatened not to divulge any information until Garrett or Chief Mateo is ready for you to know." She finishes filling the last vial and turns, putting them in a glass cooler.

"Now it's time for the ultrasound." She moves the tray and slides a machine over. So many more questions pop into my head but there's no use asking, they will just be ignored or diverted.

I lay back as she pulls up my shirt, squirting cold-ass gel onto my stomach. I hiss through my teeth. She cringes. "Sorry, I forget how cold this stuff is when it first comes out." I look at the ceiling.

Do you happen to know what the hell is going on here? I'm at a loss. Are they looking for babies or something? I don't think they'll find much.

Yeah, I'm not getting a good vibe from this one. There ARE things about this place that seem off. I'm catching a strange scent that I don't like.

What are you talking about? I don't smell anything.

Suddenly, a rush flows through me, and a new, foul scent hits my nose. My face scrunches in response. Clara looks at me.

"What's wrong? Am I pushing down too hard?"

Before I can answer, she looks at the screen, and her eyes widen for just a second before pulling herself together.

Clara clears her throat and wraps up the ultrasound equipment. "Well, I've seen all I need to see. It's time to get you back." She swiftly washes the gel off my stomach and helps me up.

I open my mouth to say something, but she rushes for the door, locking it behind her.

What the fuck was that about? And what the hell was that smell? What is happening?

Being mindful of the chains, I put my head in my hands. Then, the voice chimes in, *That's what I was talking about. I pump some of our power into you to show you something is wrong here. I can't quite put my claw on it.*

Claw?

I roll my eyes. I am so done with this shit. Everything this past year has flipped on its lid. I'm going crazy, and now the voice in my head is talking about having claws?

Suddenly, the door swings open, and Garrett marches in, his eyes a different color than before. He goes straight for me, his hands gripped into a fist, his eyes narrowed. I stand up, steeling myself, preparing for a fight.

Yanking the chain, he grabs the ankle shackles and locks them to my ankles. His normal, brooding mood had shifted to something darker.

What got into this asshat? the voice says as Garret holds the middle of the chain, pulling us toward the door.

I have no idea. Something must've happened. Do you think it has anything to do with what Clara found on the ultrasound?

I feel her shrug her shoulders at my question.

"What's wrong? Did something show up on the ultrasound or something?" It's driving me crazy not knowing.

"Don't worry about it. All you need to know is that you're going back to the cave," he grinds out, not missing a step.

I stumble a few times. Every time, he growls at me and pulls harder on the chain, but we manage to get to the cave. Garrett refastened the chain to the wall.

"Oh by the way, before you get your hopes set too high on your precious *Langdon* saving you, don't," He says Langdon's name like it's a sour taste in his mouth.

A feeling bubbles inside me, dreading what he's about to say, knowing it can't be good. I squint my eyes at him, daring him to say more. He squats, looking me dead in the eyes, a sickening smirk on his face.

"He tried and failed to protect his precious little princess. He's dead, and you will never be with him again." He laughs a sick, twisted laugh before standing.

Rage rolls inside me, and I cannot control myself. Something reaches the surface inside me, threatening to burst. "You lie! There's no way he would let you get that close to him!" He steps back, confusion evident in his gaze.

My eyes start to burn, followed by the aching in my bones, that feel like growing pains. My heartbeat speeds up, and suddenly, the chains burst as my arms grow to twice their size. Coarse brown fur starts growing all over my body, and claws take the place of my fingers, as my fury boils over.

How dare he take away the only thing that ever made my life whole?

Remember when I told you that you would find out when we're ready about who I am and what we are? The voice says gruffly.

Yes, of course I do. I've been told that a lot lately. What exactly is happening? I have some clue, as it feels like I am watching from the background. I don't understand what is going on.

I am the Kodiak side of you. Jackass here has taken what is ours, and now it's my turn to come out and play. We're going to show this son of a bitch who he is truly fucking with.

Pain slices through me as my Bear claws her way further to the surface. We triple in size, making Garrett look like a dwarf in comparison.

We catch Garrett off guard and throw him straight into the cave wall. He falls, crumpled to the floor. He doesn't stay down long. He bolts up and shifts into a Grizzly. Not quite as big as I am.

Towering over him, I swipe at him, but he dodges it. I lose my balance for a second, but quickly recover.

Where did all this come from? I've never really been a fighter, I ask as we dodge Garrett's sad attempt to swipe back.

It's always been inside you. I've always been a part of you. It wasn't until we met our mate, Langdon, that I appeared.

So, that's why I felt so strongly for him so quickly.

Before I can say or think another word, Garrett takes advantage of my being distracted and grabs my neck from behind, wrapping his arms around me in a chokehold. He moves so fast we trip and fall, landing with him on top and overpowering us.

Chapter Twelve

LANGDON

I crouch in the brush as I hide from the tribe I had been with for a year. Most of them walk around as if nothing in the world could hurt them. But they are wrong. The most dangerous person among them is me.

"I thought you were going to wait for me by the cave?" Gracie's voice sounds over my shoulder.

"Shhh. Are you fucking crazy? We are deep into enemy territory, and you want to come up behind someone and scream?" I hush her as I turn on her and slap my hand over her mouth. "What did my father say?"

She pushes my hand away from her mouth and growls. "He said he will be here soon. But you are going to have to have patience and wait for backup."

"Ugh. We are going to do some reconnaissance. You take the right side, and I'll take the left. Don't make contact with anyone," I counter with a glare.

"You know he is going to be even more upset with you if you make a mess of things here."

"What is that supposed to mean?" I snap at her in a whisper.

"He's pissed that you didn't call earlier about what happened. Your mother has been mourning your death because you stopped sending her letters."

I never meant to hurt her, but I couldn't let her know that I was still alive if I was going to make sure that the Grizzlies didn't find out I was Kodiak

I roll my eyes and turn away from Gracie, leaving her to follow my instructions. "Just don't get caught."

I continue around the perimeter. My mind going back to what they tried to do to Georgie before they took her from me. Their chief has taken what is mine, and I am here to get my mate back.

Rounding the tribe to where the doctor's small cabin sits, I do not make a sound. Clara is one of the only bears here that I think I can trust. At the end of the day, she is the only one who knows what everyone who comes to her has been through. All I hope is that I am able to get in and find what I need.

It isn't as busy on this side of the territory. Since it looks like they are celebrating something in the middle of the territory. Georgie's scent catches my attention, and my stomach falls as I realize they have brought her to Clara. What's happened to her? Is she sick? Did they hurt her?

If they touch a hair on her head, we will ensure none of them live. My bear is furious as I sneak into the bathroom window, which is always unlocked.

I know, and we both know that Mateo is behind this.

Dropping onto the removable wood flooring I squat and listen before heading to the door to make sure no one is with me. I open the bathroom door and scan the hallway before making my way to her office.

Georgie's scent leads me to a room with an ultrasound machine, which has something hanging out of it. Going to it, I pull the paper off and see two blobs on it. I glance at the name, and I'm floored. Georgie is fucking pregnant!

Clara's scent comes to me, and I turn just as she enters the room, the ultrasound photo clenched in my hand. She gasps when she notices that it's me standing in the room.

"Where is the woman that you did this ultrasound on?" I stalk up to her. My bear taking over my mind and body in the process. He is pissed that she is now somewhere on this territory, carrying our cubs.

"She is fine, and yes, she is pregnant. I've been giving her extra food when I can," Clara stammers as I back her into the wall.

"I asked you—where she is!" I snarl at her. If she doesn't tell me where she is soon, I am going to do something that I wouldn't normally do in my right mind.

My bear is striving to take over, and I don't know if I'm able to keep control over this situation. Clara whimpers under my aura as I growl at her. "Does anyone else know about the cubs?"

Clara whines louder in front of me. I'm going to be livid if she's told anyone about this. She finally nods, and I lose it. Grabbing her up by her scrubs, I bring her face-to-face with me.

"Who!" I growl in her face, spittle flying from my mouth splashing into her face.

"I had no other choice! Garrett is of a higher rank. I couldn't go against his wishes!" Clara stutters.

"You better hope that he doesn't hurt her or them. If he does, *YOU* will go down with them. No matter how nice you were to me when I was here. If they are hurt, I'll blame you." I fist the ultrasound in my hand and take a step away from her before I kill her right here and now. "Tell me where my mate is, now."

"She is in a cave. I'll take you." She keeps her gaze on the floor as she speaks to me. With the aura I'm projecting, there is no way she can look me in the eyes.

"Then, get walking. I want to know where my mate is."

Sounds of roars and thuds come from outside. My heart accelerates, thinking that Gracie is out there already fighting with the tribe.

I run outside and realize this bear isn't Gracie but Georgie.

Fuck, she is beautiful as she stands on her hind feet, towering over them all. Another bear runs up behind her as she roars at the ones in front of her. Sprinting out to her, I shift quickly, dropping the ultrasound in the process, and crash into the oncoming bear. We both fly back and roll down the hill before hitting a tree.

The crunch as the other bear hits the tree tells me that he won't be getting up. A snap of a twig beside me catches my attention. Gracie stands still, in shock, as her eyes go to the bear and then me.

"I thought I told you not to start this fight? Are you crazy, there are only two of us!" Gracie shouts as she stalks forward.

Shifting back to my human form, I square up to Gracie. My arms over my chest as we stare at each other. "I didn't start this. If we are going to continue this right here, Georgie won't make it. She is the one up that hill fighting the other bears."

Gracie's features change at the mention of her friend, and she steps back from me. "You mean she's up there? She shifted?"

"Yes, now shift and help me help her until my dad gets here." Gracie nods, and we both change.

We race up the hill, our massive paws shaking the ground under our weight. Georgie is still fighting the other bears when I spot Garrett in his bear form. He looks the worse for wear as he charges at the massive bear in the center of the territory.

I race forward, leaving Gracie in my wake. He isn't going to hurt my mate anymore. Using my shoulder and weight, I throw him off course. The bear stands to his feet and turns his head to me.

Garrett doesn't know it is me because I've never shifted in front of him. Hell, for the year that I was here, I never shifted in front of anyone. So to them, I'm as much of an enemy as Gracie and Georgie. The only way that he is going to know who I am. Is to mind-link with him.

I will kill you for hurting her! I growl in his head. The shock that comes from him before he growls out loud makes me smirk in my head.

I knew there was something weird about you! There was no way that you would have the strength to fight full-grown bears in your human form! What tribe are you from? Garrett is pissed and nervous at the same time.

Let's just say that you and Chief Mateo have incurred the wrath of the biggest Kodiak tribe in

Alaska. Because not only did you almost kill me, you have hurt the heir to the chief's mate and I'm going to kill you, I snarl and lunge forward.

Garrett doesn't back down and charges at me. I'm going to kill him, what I told him isn't a threat; it's a promise. He and Chief Mateo will no longer be part of this earth once I finish with them.

Using my massive paw, I swipe at Garrett's head, snapping it to the side. Blood spills from his cheek as he turns his glowing eyes on me. He doesn't have a chance. I'm the heir of a powerful tribe. A strong tribe that he and his chief had pissed off.

Garrett rushes me, and I stand on my hind legs with a roar. The rumble of the ground informs me that Gracie has finally ascended the hill. I don't take my eyes off the bear in front of me. The only thing I hope is that she is able to help Georgie.

With fury, I come down on top of the bear in front of me. Digging my claws in his back and scoring them up to his head. Garrett roars in pain as I tunnel them into shoulder blades and throw him into a building. The entire building caves in on top of him, and I turn to see Gracie and Georgie fighting with two other bears. Protecting each other's backs.

Chief Mateo rushes toward the girls. I push myself to full speed and grab his left back leg with my teeth. Pulling him away from them, the ground begins to shudder, bringing my attention to my right. My father is leading an enormous company of bears into the territory. Each of them huge beasts as they shoulder past brush and grizzlies as they charge forward with teeth bared.

Mateo stiffens before trying to tear his leg from my mouth. He finally frees his leg and blood pools on my tongue as I chase after him. I catch up with him and tear into his hindquarters, leaving deep punctures right before his hip. Mateo roars at me and swipes his paw at my face.

A nail grazes my left eye, sending blood down my face as I try to make out where he is from my right. I fling my head, trying to get rid of the blood, but it continues its sticky flow from my eye and into my fur.

Mateo plows into me, sending me crashing into something hard. I slowly get up, and I'm able to move when he rushes me again. Grabbing hold of his ear, I tear it clean off and fling it to the ground as he roars in pain. The way he bares his teeth and lunges for me, tells me I need to finish this quickly.

Taking hold of his muzzle, I crush it between my teeth and toss him to the side. Mateo can hardly whimper as I make my way over to him to end him once and for all. Standing on my hind legs, I drop down onto his pathetic, broken body. My front paws land on his face crushing his skull over and over until he is dead.

Chapter Thirteen

GEORGINNA

This has to end. I was starting to wear out. Never in my life did I ever think I would end up in an all-out battle, let alone in a battle as a bear. Why do these bears, whom I tower over, by the way, have such a damn problem with me? I've never done anything to them.

A paw swings at me, and I deflect with ease, missing me by a mile. I back up and hit something huge. A familiar scent catches my attention. I turn around to find Gracie in bear form. There's no time for greetings, another bear comes at me.

Back-to-back with Gracie, we fight off Grizzlies left, right, and center. Holy fucking hell, how many bears are in this tribe?

It's a whole fucking tribe. Generally, Grizzlies are solitary animals, but I guess food has been scarce for them because it looks as though there are around fifty bears here, my bear informs me, not missing a beat.

Another bear comes up and bites into my side.

AAARRRGGG, we grind out before throwing the offending Grizzly off us. As soon as we get rid of one, another comes at us. I easily paw it away, and he collides with a tree.

Are you okay, Georgie? Gracie says at my back, still fending off the others. *I mean, of course you are, you're here fighting. Sorry, that was a moronic question.* I laugh. Leave it to Gracie to bring humor in a perilous situation.

How am I able to hear Gracie? I throw another bear aside.

It is called mind-linking. That is what shifters do when they have a bond. Since you and Gracie are blood-cousins, you are able to hear each other even though you do not talk out loud, my bear answers.

Of course! One more piece of information to add to the never-ending pile. I roll my eyes.

"Garrett said he killed Langdon. Is that true?" *Oh God, I hope not. That would break me even more.* She throws a bear into a tree and turns to me.

"No, it's not true. It sounds like you just wanted to get under your skin," she says without moving her lips. I shove another bear away, careering him down the hill.

Just then, I see Langdon going after what appears to be the head of the tribe.

HE IS ALIVE!

Oh, thank fuck!

I look behind him and see the rubble of what used to be a building, a bear lying dead, presumably Garrett. Someone climbs on my back, biting down on my shoulder blade. I reach back, throwing him down in front of me, and stomp as hard as I can above him, crushing his skull in.

Damn! I didn't know I could be so violent, I say amazed.

Well, actually, that's all thanks to me, my bear chimes in. *I can help heighten your senses. That's what shifters do. They draw on their animal side to help in certain situations.*

Of course, she's her feisty self.

Okay, thank you for the clarity.

She laughs. It feels like she has been laughing at me quite a lot lately.

"Georgie!" I hear Langdon call my name. I turn to see him running toward me. The other bear dead on the ground behind him. Looking around, all the Grizzlies are immobile—deceased and no longer a threat. I turn around in time for Langdon to wrap me in his embrace. We hold each other as we shift back into our human forms.

"You're alive!" I say into his chest, his chest hair tickling my nose. The beating of his heart slows to an even pace as we stand.

"Of course I'm alive. No one is going to stop me from getting to you. I'm just relieved that you're alive and well." I look up at him, a look crosses his face, one I cannot decipher. His hands grab the sides of my face and pull me into a deep, sensual kiss and the world melts away. And at this moment, all that I can feel is Langdon.

"Okay, you love birds. I hate to break up this lovely reunion, but we need to figure out what to do next." Gracie interrupts, a hint of humor in her voice.

"Why were they after me? What do they want? Garrett said my name was Rowan and they thought they got rid of all the Rowans." I look back at Gracie. I've known her my entire life. She will know any and everything about my family.

"Do you know what he meant, Grace?" A look of guilt crosses her face, and she gazes at Langdon and then back at me.

What am I missing? I fucking hate being left in the dark.

Suddenly, someone emerges seemingly out of nowhere and scares the shit out of me. "You must be Georginna. It's a pleasure to meet you," a burly, older man says. He looks like an older version of Lang.

"I'm sorry... who are you?" I ask.

He laughs a loud, gravelly laugh and steps closer. "I apologize. I'm Archer. I am the leader of the Kodiak tribe and Langdon's father." He looks at Langdon. "We don't have much time. I managed to capture that lowlife, Garrett, and have him held in one of the caves. He should come soon. We need to hurry and question him before time runs out."

Langdon nods and turns back to me. "Let's go get those answers. I have clothes in what's left of my tent we can change into." He pulls me toward a tent that is left half-standing. He throws one of his T-shirts and sweatpants my way, and we hurry to change so we can meet the others at the cave.

We reach the cave, and Garrett is chained up at the far end, much like I was when he brought me here.

Karma's a bitch. I laugh. Lang turns to me and smiles. "What's so funny?"

"I was just thinking that karma has struck so nicely." He laughs, wrapping an arm around me. It warms my heart to hear that sound again.

We get closer to Garrett, Archer kicks him hard in the side. "Wake up you piece of shit," he bellows.

Garrett grunts and looks up, squinting. "You have no idea who you are fucking with. When the rest of the tribe hears what you've done, you are all finished," Garrett tells him, then spits at his feet.

Archer bends down and grabs him by the throat, lifting him in the air, the chain dangling in front of him. "Listen here, you little shit, the only one who is finished here is you if you don't cooperate with us and give us the answers we seek." Archer drops him hard on his side.

Garrett slowly rolls himself to sitting and looks straight at me. "Looks like you found your way, Rowan. Don't get too comfortable. We aren't the only ones looking for you."

I cross my arms. He doesn't scare me much anymore, but of course, the idea of others coming after me scares the shit out of me. What did I do to deserve all of this hatred?

Langdon rushes forward, grips Garrett's throat before throwing him against the wall, knocking him out. Lang stands there looking murderous and staring at him.

Archer walks behind Lang and puts a hand on his shoulder. "Langdon, my son. We need him alive to question him. He's no good to us dead. He's trying to get a rise out of you and Georginna. Do not give in."

Archer takes a step back as I move toward Lang. His death grip on Garrett still intact. He doesn't seem to let up. Wrapping my arms around him, I try my best to appeal to him. "Please don't kill him yet. Like your father said, we need answers ." I look up at him, my chin resting on his chest.

He holds me close and kisses my forehead. "I know, my sweet Georgie. I just can't stand him talking to you like that. He's done so much to hurt you. I just want him to end." Movement comes behind me, and I turn. Garrett is slowly coming to.

Chapter Fourteen

LANGDON

Georgie looks beside us, bringing my attention to the asshole in chains by the wall. Garrett slowly comes round where I threw him against the rocky interior. It's him and this tribe that has caused all the harm to my mate, and I have every intention to make him pay.

Mateo got off easy, but now Garrett will have to take the brunt of my anger. I'll be damned if my father keeps me from protecting what's mine. *He would do the same for my mother.

Garrett glances around, measuring us all up. After being with the tribe with him for a year, I have learned his ways. The nervousness in his eyes tells me that he knows he isn't a match for all of us.

Walking over to Garrett, leaving Georgie next to my father, I squat just out of his reach. I stare at him, my bear rising from inside of me, urging me to rip him limb from limb to protect what is ours. Garrett lowers his eyes from mine since he is a lower-ranked bear than me.

"So, Garrett, are you going to talk? Or just sit here and die a slow death in these chains?" I snarl. I'm tired of playing his games. He is going to tell me what I want to know. Even if I have to use my bear's aura to make him. "Why did this tribe kill the Rowan Kodiak tribe?"

"Because they had what we wanted. At least, that is what Chief Mateo thought." The evil glint in his eyes as they travel from me to Georgie and then back again has my bear clawing to get out.

"Okay, what did they have? Tell me why what they had that cost the entire tribe's death." He is doing the same thing with me again. Giving me bits and pieces but not revealing everything.

"The only thing I've overheard is that the object would be protected. Possibly hidden from outsiders. Whatever it was, it would make the tribe the strongest of all bears." His gaze now fixes on Georgie.

I turn from Garrett to look at my mate. Her eyebrows pinch together, trying to make sense of everything. Behind her stands Gracie, her bear's eyes flashing, baring her teeth at the man on the ground. I pull my eyes from her and bring them back to Garrett.

"Where did you find this information? And why did your tribe think it was the Rowans?"

"We got it from one of their own elders."

"Where is this elder now?"

The malicious smirk that graces his face can only suggest that the information he has isn't good.

"They are no longer on this plane. Once we were done, we did away with him. He thought that he was going to be the leader of the new Kodiak tribe. To take the only living chieftain female and breed the best tribe."

The growl that echoes off the walls of the cave makes me realize it has come from me. I have my hands around his throat before I know it. Garrett's fingers dig into my hands. I don't even notice his nails cutting into my flesh as he struggles. Hands grasp all over me, but the ones I feel the most are Georgie's.

She holds my forearms, trying to force me to let him go. My bear's strength and my own cause Garrett to go from a flesh color to a dark red. His lips are turning blue, and his eyes begin to turn red from the lack of oxygen.

"Lang! We still need information! Stop!" Her voice finally pulls me out of the anger-induced blackout. My bear recedes deep inside of me as I allow her to pull my hands away from Garrett's throat.

The reflection of my eyes in hers doesn't surprise me. My bear's eyes are the last to leave from the surface. Taking in a deep breath, I try to calm myself to be able to continue my interrogation of this fuckwit.

"I'm fine, Georgie." My fingers softly run over her cheek. She leans into the caress as her eyes flutter before glancing up at me.

"We need to take precautions tonight. Then, we will take Garrett and those who attacked and are loyal to him back to our tribe and try them."

My father's voice catches my attention to him and Gracie.

"Why not try them here?" Georgie asks beside me.

"Because it is tribal law that digressions against a Kodiak tribe. The bear or bears are then tried by a Kodiak tribe. Since ours is the only one left after they wiped out the Rowan tribe, it falls on us to get justice for our friends." my father explains. I know he'd want to bring them back to our tribe.

Besides, it would be good to get Georgie under the protection of my tribe rather than have to worry about something else happening to her while we are by ourselves. I'm sure my mother would love to see me and dote on Georgie.

"Okay, Father, then we leave in the morning. Did you bring enough to handle the prisoners?"

"Son, I don't come to a battle half-assed." He grins back at me before leaving the cave.

I grab Georgie's hand and lead her out of the cave. Garrett doesn't make a move or sound as Gracie growls at him and follows us. My father places guards at the entrance. No one will be getting past them. Both bears have been in the tribe for years, but you would never know exactly how old they are.

The thing about being in a tribe like mine is we are close. To humans, we are just another town, but they never come into it. We don't like it when people come to our territory. Which is why we have such incredible guards.

"Lang, is something wrong?" Georgie's voice brings me out of my thoughts about my tribe. If I'm being honest, I miss them all.

"Just thinking, Georgie," I answer her, bringing her hand to my lips and placing a kiss on the back of it.

"What are you thinking about?"

Sighing, I turn around as I notice some of the tribe have made the trek to help even though I have been gone for a few years.

"Thinking about what it would be like to lead this tribe with you by my side."

My eyes lock with hers as the other tribe members bring more of the fighters from Mateo's tribe to the cave. I can't help to notice the want in her eyes as we stand in the middle of the trail. Glancing around, I take off with her hand in mine.

Father has this, they are his tribe until I decide that I want to take over. But it looks like I will be sooner than later. It has been a few days since me and Georgie have been together, and I know just the place to have her before we have to take the rest of this rag tag company back to my home.

"Lang, where are we going?" I don't miss the giggle in her voice as we crash through some bushes.

"I found a lake and want to show it to you." I don't just want to show it to her, but I want to experience it with her.

We finally leave the trail and forest. The sparkling light blue lake looms before us as we walk over to it. I release her hand and begin to strip out of the clothes I put on in my tent. Pulling off the pants, I notice the ultrasound in the front pocket, where I had stuffed them after shifting back.

I don't want to ask her about it yet, knowing that they probably haven't told her about the babies. Her shifting while pregnant was a risk, but she had to protect herself because I couldn't get to her quickly enough.

"Lang, what are you doing?" I look up and spot the pink in her cheeks brightening.

"We are going for a swim. Take those clothes off unless you want to get them wet," I answer her as I stuff the ultrasound back in my pocket and approach her.

Georgie stares at me as I stop in front of her. I can tell she is nervous since this is the first time we have been together out in the open. My body hums as I hook my fingers in the edge of her shirt and pull up. She lifts her arms above her head, allowing me to take it over her head.

I groan as her breasts bounce free of the cotton shirt. Ever since meeting her, I could tell that we were made for each other. I just didn't know that she was my mate until her bear started to come forward. If we had met while I was still at my tribe, and hers hadn't been decimated, things probably would have been different.

The soft sigh from Georgie has me squatting and bringing the pants down her shapely legs. A whimper leaves her mouth as her hands flex at her sides. I run my hands over her ass and then up her back.

"Lang..." she moans my name as I lean forward to allow my lips to touch her pussy.

I trail the flat of my tongue across her inner thigh, making my way back up to her quivering core. The arousal coming from her begs me to take her right here and now instead of in the lake. Georgie's hands go into my hair and fist it as I clamp my lips on her clit and suck, changing the pressure while I knead the back of her thighs.

"Lang, someone is going to see us." I barely hear her with my attention is on her pussy.

I glance up and notice that she is staring at me with hooded eyes. Her cheeks turn crimson and get darker as I stare back at her while my lips are wrap around her clit. Popping off, I pick her up and walk with her in my arms to the lake.

Georgie squeals as I plunge us into the cool water. Her legs wrap around my hips. The only reason we don't freeze is our bears keeping us warmer than the average human. She climbs higher in my arms as I walk to the middle so the water covers us.

I kiss her with her arousal on my lips, her moan making me harder than ever before. Hell, it might also be that she is carrying my cubs in her belly, and she doesn't even know it.

"I want you, Georgie. Let me have you?"

She nods with her lips touching mine. I back up against a boulder and pull her body over my cock. Sheathing it with her warm pussy brings a groan up and out of my mouth as she tightens around me.

"Fuck, Georgie. You're so tight right now."

Georgie's nails bite into my shoulder blades as I thrust into her, making the water sway with each one. I know that once we finish, we will have to talk about the cubs, but right now I just need to feel her and be inside her.

"Lang, right there. Don't... Stop..." she moans in my ear.

She is tightening around me, milking me with each pulse, but I don't want to come before her. Georgie nips my neck and meets me with each thrust as I get closer and closer.

"Come for me, Georgie, come with me," I beg her.

"I'm coming, Lang!" she screams.

Chapter Fifteen

GEORGINNA

For the first time in over a year, I am finally happy. I have Langdon back and although new information would usually overwhelm me, it has given me a sense of freedom. Relief had flown through me when I realized that the voice in my head was a part of me that had been hidden away my entire life.

Langdon kisses the top of my head as we lay on the bank of the lake in post-coital bliss. He sits beside me, and I join him. A look crosses his face, it seems like he's wrestling with something.

"What's wrong?" I ask, putting my hand on his arm.

He turns, grabbing both my hands. "I found out something today when I went looking for you. I followed your scent to the doctor's tent..." I think back to when I was at Clara's office. I stare at him. He clears his throat. "It turns out, you're pregnant with my cubs."

My eyes widen. *Cubs*? I'm at a loss for words. I open and close my mouth too many times to count.

How? When? Cubs, as in bears? So many questions, it's hard to wrap my brain around.

He grabs my face and brings my attention to him. The face splitting grin I see on his face tells me everything I need to know. "Don't worry," he chuckles, "they are going to be normal healthy *human* babies. I know this is a lot for you to get your pretty head around, but we can talk about all of that later. I want you to be careful. With you expecting, you are more vulnerable. I would die if something happened to you and our babies."

He places my hands on his bare chest. Did he just say what I think he just said?

Standing, I stare down at him. "Wait, what do you mean by "babies"? I'm going to need you to clarify that. How many babies am I going to have?!" Now I'm definitely freaking out. How am I going to handle multiple babies?

He stands and wraps me in his embrace, laughing. Is he seriously laughing at me? Lifting my head, he looks into my eyes.

"Don't worry, we can do this. I'm here and will be every step of the way." He turns and bends down, reaching for something in his pants pocket. He pulls out a small, shiny piece of paper. "When I went searching for you, I snuck into Clara's office, following your scent. I found this sticking out of the machine." He hands me what he's holding.

This must've been why she ran out of the room and why Garrett was so pissed off about it. Did they know before he brought me to her office?

I stare at the image, trying to make sense of it. It's a black-and-white image with two peanut shapes floating in the middle.

"This is *my* ultrasound?" I clutch the picture to my chest as tears run down my face. He reaches up and wipes them away, wrapping me in a hug.

We stand in each other's arms for what feels like forever.

I cannot believe I'm pregnant, and not only that, but I'm going to have twins. Do twins run in my family? I don't think so. I'm going to have to talk to Gracie and find out. She's older and knows more about my ancestry than apparently I do.

Langdon kisses the top of my head. "We should catch up with the rest of the tribe. We have a lot to discuss." I nod, and we get dressed and head toward the camp center.

Once we get to the camp, I spot Gracie and race over for a hug. Langdon catches up with the other Kodiaks.

"I'm so glad you're alright. I'm so sorry I wasn't there for you." Her eyes start to water.

"I'm good. Don't worry about it." Charlie pops into my head. Oh shit! "What about Charlie? How is he? Last I saw, he was lying in a pool of blood."

I grip her arms, hoping for some good news. Please tell me he's all right. I would lose it if he didn't survive. She smiles, which is a good sign.

"He's fine. He is resting in the cabin. Langdon and I found him. I tended to him while Langdon came up with a plan to save you."

Returning her smile, I let out a breath and wrap her in a relieved hug.

"I'm so glad everything turned out alright. I have some news." I pull away and take the ultrasound out of my pocket, showing it to her. Her eyes widen and her head shoots up, her hands gripping the paper. I smile and nod, tears welling in my eyes.

"Are you serious?!" She rushes at me, almost knocking me down. Laughing, I quickly recover. She pulls back; a worried expression crosses her face. Then, she looks back at the ultrasound, getting a closer look.

Yep, I know that look. She's just noticing that there are more than one little peanuts. I take her hand as she looks up at me. "Yes, there are two little ones there. Langdon called them 'cubs,'" I tell her with a smile.

I swear, I haven't smiled this much in such a long time. I didn't think I would ever truly be able to smile again after what happened to Langdon. My life has truly changed in the past couple of weeks.

I found Langdon alive, got kidnapped, and not only found out that my 'family' wasn't who I thought they were, but I also came to find out that I am a Kodiak shifter. And to top it all off, I'm pregnant with twins!

How is this seriously my life?

Speaking of my family...

"Grace, where are we originally from? I always thought we were from Hobart, but in light of current events, I seriously doubt anything I thought I knew."

Guilt crosses her face, telling me she hasn't been truthful with me. When I think things are starting to look up for me, something comes along and reminds me that my life is screwed up. I take a deep breath and cross my arms over my chest. "Just tell me, Gracie. Now is your chance to get everything you've been 'shielding' me from. I'm tired of all the lies and secrets. This ends now."

Taking a steadying breath, she nods. "Okay, but just so you know, I didn't do any of it to hurt you. We just wanted to help you." I return her nod, trying my best to keep an open mind.

Given all that has happened, I know Gracie would never want to hurt me. "Go on," I urge her to continue.

"To answer your question, no... we are not from Hobart. We aren't even from the mainland USA. We both were born and raised in the Kodiak Island Borough in Alaska..." She pauses.

So, wait, I was born in Alaska? How the hell do I not remember?

"So, how old was I when we moved here? Why did we move? Was anything Garrett said true!?"

I feel as though I'm a stranger in my own body. Everything was fine before Garrett barreled into my life. I was blissfully unaware of what my life supposedly was, and now...

"You were three years old, and I was seven when we moved here. Your mom, my aunt, entrusted me to look after you and find friends of theirs—your parents—to care for us in Hobart. Yes, what Garrett said about our family is true. We moved so you would be safe. Everyone in the tribe was murdered, including my parents and your dad."

All of a sudden, I feel the urge to sit down before my legs give out. So the parents I adored and loved weren't really my parents? Don't get me wrong, I wouldn't trade them for anything, but what about my mom?

"Why didn't my mom just take me? Why did she stay behind?" I sit on the ground next to a tree. I look over at Langdon, in deep conversation with his father. I'm assuming they're coming up with a plan.

"Aunt Aria was wounded and couldn't make the trip. I don't know if she ever made it out alive. She knew her best shot was to have me and one surviving elder take you far away from the borough so you and I would be safe. After the elder dropped us off at Junie and Micheal's, our foster parent's house, he left. I haven't heard from him since. I heard recently, though, that your mom may have been spotted in her bear form. But that hasn't been confirmed."

I rest my head against the tree and look up at the sky. Gracie sits next to me. "I'm sorry to drop all this on you, Georgie. I figured if I'm going to tell you, I may as well tell the *whole* story." Reaching for her hand, I hold it in mine, resting it on my knee. "It's definitely a lot to take in all at once. But I'm glad you told me." I try to think back to my childhood.

Was there any clue that my life was weird in any way? No. It was great. We went on trips, I got into some trouble, which Grace helped me out of, and we went camping numerous times.

My brows form a *V* as I lift my head from the tree, looking into the woods. Thinking back to when I was a teenager, about thirteen. There was one bear that I saw practically every time we went camping...

"Georginna, honey, we need you to help Gracie gather sticks for the campfire if you want s'mores," Mom says as she and my dad set up camp.

"Mmkay. Gracie!" I shouted to my cousin who was crouching behind a tree, seeming to be looking for something. She must be concentrating heavily on whatever she's looking for. She hasn't heard me. I walk up to her. "Gracie," I call again. This time, she jumps, and I laugh until my cheeks hurt. She stands, shoving my arm, making me go backward slightly.

"Don't do that. You scared the crap out of me." I stifle my grin and clear my throat. "Sorry. Mom wants us to gather sticks for the fire." She nods, and we head further into the woods.

Walking back to camp with an arm full of sticks and thick branches, I sense that I'm being watched. I stop suddenly, Gracie bumps into my back, dropping the sticks.

"What the... What are you stopping for?" she asks as she picks up the sticks she dropped.

"Shhhh," I answer, trying to see if I could hear anyone.

Looking around, I spot a bear. I haven't seen any bears like that around here before. It is huge and brown, like a grizzly but much bigger. I need to look up what kind of bear it is. "Sorry, I thought I heard something. Come on, let's go get ready to make some s'mores."

Sitting at the campfire, I watch, amazed as the marshmallow starts to brown on the stick. Personally, I like my marshmallow burned. It gives the s'mores added flavor. My eyes are caught by a pair of eyes watching me. For some reason, it doesn't scare me. Those eyes seem to be familiar.

We arrive home the next day. After powering up the computer, I pull up the search engine and type in, "What brown bears are bigger than grizzly bears?" Pictures of big brown bears pop up; they look just like the bears I saw in the woods.

Under the picture reads: "Kodiak bears are the largest bears in the world..." Reading further, I find that they come from Alaska.

Staring at the computer, my brows knit together. Alaska? If they come from Alaska, what is that one doing here in Hobart, Oklahoma?

I guess the answer to my question came about fifteen years later. I look over just in time to see Langdon walking toward me. Pushing myself to stand, I brace my hand against the tree as I steady myself before standing straight.

"Are you okay?" he asks as he reaches me, concern marring his handsome face.

I smile at him. "I'm good. I was just reminiscing about my childhood. I was thinking about the time I went camping; a Kodiak bear was watching me. I was never scared of it like most kids would be. I somehow felt protected. I never understood it until now. What if that bear was somehow someone from our tribes?"

His eyebrows shoot up. "When did you start seeing this bear?"

"I first saw it when I was thirteen," I tell him about the encounter and how I felt then. His brows knit together.

"It can't be..." he said so quietly I almost didn't hear him.

"What is it?" I grab his arms. Does he know something I don't?

He turns to Gracie. "Are you sure her mom and dad died?" he questions, but she looks dumbfounded.

"Her dad, yes..." She takes a deep breath before continuing, "I saw him take his last breath when I was hiding under the table. But the last that I saw of Aunt Aria, she was wounded, and I wasn't sure if she would make it. So, no, I don't know for a fact that she died."

It feels like the wind has been knocked out of me.

Could my birth mother really be alive? If so, where has she been all these years?

Those are questions that need answering.

Chapter Sixteen

LANGDON

I watch across the field as Gracie talks with Georgie beside a tree. Whatever she is saying has Georgie sliding down the tree that she is next to, her hand running through her hair. I pat a tribe member on the shoulder and walk over to them.

Georgie stands, and Gracie turns to glance back over at me as I walk up to the pair. "Are you okay?"

"I'm good. I was reminiscing about my childhood. I was thinking about the time I went camping, there was a Kodiak bear there, watching me. I was never scared of it like any other kid would be. I somehow felt protected. I never understood it until now. What if that bear was somehow someone from our tribes?" She smiles sweetly at me before telling me about a memory that she had with Gracie and her adoptive parents.

"When did you see this bear?" I want to know to give me a timeline to ask my father. Maybe he sent someone out here to keep an eye on things? Maybe he knew that she was still alive?

"I first saw it when I was thirteen," she tells me before beginning to tell me how she felt and the way the encounter occurred.

"It can't be..." I shake my head. Why would she not come forward after knowing everything was okay? Could she still be alive? Or is it someone else?

"What is it?" She grabs my arms. Her eyes searching mine, trying to find something in them to tell her what I know.

"Are you sure her mom and dad died?" I question, turning to Gracie, who looks dumbfounded. I know that it takes a lot to kill one of us. Which is why Garret used a gun on me.

"Her dad, yes..." She takes a deep breath before continuing, "I saw him take his last breath when I was hiding under the table. But the last that I saw of Aunt Aria; she was wounded; I wasn't sure if she would make it. So, no, I don't know for a fact that she died."

"We need to talk to my dad about this. It needs to be private, so we must return to the tribe. I don't want anyone in the Grizzlies to know that more than one Rowan may still be alive."

They both nod, and I take Georgie's hand, bringing her to my side and up to the other Kodiaks. If she is going to be part of the community, she will need to get acquainted with them. Because I'm sure now that my father knows my whereabouts, he will want me to take over as tribal leader. And I'm not going to do that without Georgie by my side.

"Guys this is Georginna, my mate, and her cousin, Gracie. They will be joining us on our way home. I don't want anything to happen to them. You guys understand?" They all nod and come forward to shake their hands. The only thing another male can do to a mated female.

Gracie is the first to introduce herself. Most of the males are unmated, but she doesn't even bat an eye.

Having more eyes on them means I will be less stressed along the journey. Well, until we make our detour to the cabin. They would never go against an order from a chief—even if he is still just the heir.

We leave the group of males and head over to my father. I need to talk with him. It is getting late in the day, and I don't want to keep Georgie here much longer, especially with all the prisoners we have.

"Father, when are we leaving?" He looks up from his seat on the boulder where he is talking with one of the warriors.

"In the cover of darkness. It will be best to move this number of bears in the dark. If the humans were to see us, it would cause issues for the other shifters that have made their home here in the States." I nod; at least we won't be here much longer. Once I have Georgie and the cubs where we are safe, I will feel much better.

I also want to talk with my parents about the annihilation of Georgie's tribe and to discover whether any of the others survived. The only thing is, if there are some alive, they will have to come under our banner since Georgie is my mate.

Otherwise, we will renounce ourselves and live on our own. Which isn't a bad idea. All of us—Georgie, the cubs, and me—at the cabin on our own. But I will cross that bridge when I come to it.

"Okay. We'll be ready to go by dusk then," I answer him and bow my head. Even though I'm his son, I still show him the respect he deserves. Well, some. It would have been more respectful if I didn't leave to go to the continental states.

But then, I wouldn't have met my mate. My Georgie. My one and only. And I wouldn't have my cubs coming into this world. Pulling Georgie with me, we go to the doctor's tent.

"Are you both hungry?" I glance between them. I know that if I'm hungry, they have to be. Especially since Georgie shifted for the first time and with her baking our twins.

"I'm famished," Georgie groans as she sits down on the tree benches in front of the tent.

"Me too. What are you going to cook up for us?" I grin and grab some wood from the doctor's tent to build a fire. One of the things I've learned in the past year is to prepare a juicy trout.

As the sun hides behind the mountains, my father's tribe begins to pack up what they have brought with them. I grab some extra clothes from the doctor's tent, making sure that we all have clothes in case I need to shift on the fly. Georgie and Gracie talk and giggle as I fling the bag over my shoulder.

It is nice seeing Georgie so happy. I can't wait to show her the tribe land I grew up in. Show her the fishing spots with the most fish. Take her up the snowy mountain trails and play in the snow.

So much to show her, but I have plenty of time to take her everywhere on the island. To show the cubs where to hide to keep away from their mother, play in the water, and swim with sea otters. Sometimes I can't believe I left there.

"Are you ready, ladies?" Georgie and Gracie turn to me and nod before extinguishing the fire.

I'm ready to have my life with Georgie and our cubs, no matter where we decide to live. They both come up to me, and I reach out for Georgie's hand, which she places in mine. Our eyes lock, and my heartbeat increases. I love her so much; she makes my heart swell.

"Ready! Let's get this tribe on the road." Georgie's smile and the bounce in her step make me excited.

My father has all the prisoners in the middle of the tribal warriors. I stand at the front with Georgie, and Gracie stands to the side as we wait for everyone to get in a line. A few warriors are in their bear forms, lining the sides of the group of prisoners.

"My fellow tribesmen. Tonight, we are heading home. We will be going through land that humans inhabit. Those in bear form will need to stick to the tree line but close enough to make sure our new friends make it up to Kodiak Island with us." My father's deep timbre makes everyone stay silent and pay attention. "As we head north, keep an eye on your surroundings. It is close to hunting season, and I'd hate for more of our tribe to be buried in this land."

Everyone nods. My father motions for the tribe to move forward and everyone hitches their bags over their shoulders. I gesture for Georgie and Gracie to follow me. It is going to be slow moving with this large number of bears..

I just hope that there won't be too many humans along our route. Georgie, Gracie, and I will be going to my cabin to retrieve Charlie. That is going to be one hell of a conversation.

Hey, bud we are going on a road trip. But you have to walk, and you might just see some crazy shit. Oh, and by the way we are bear shifters.

Not a hard conversation at all. Yeah, right.

I don't know why Gracie is dating him. Since she knows he is human, and she is a shifter. I mean, there have been bears who took a human mate in our tribe. But my father rarely allows them to stay in the tribe's territory. It is still done, though.

The next morning, we stop in a secluded field big enough hold our group. We are able to get a few hours of sleep, but then Georgie, Gracie, and I will head out before the group to get Charlie. It is nice and cool under the shelter of the trees. The silence is nothing unusual since the smaller animals can tell that we are top of the food chain. Even being in human form. they know we aren't what we appear to be. I have the distinct feeling of being followed, but I chalk it up to the fact that other animals inhabit these woods.

Continuing through, we stop at the edge of the river to freshen up and refill our water bottles. I stand watch to make sure none of the wildlife tries to hurt the girls. My bear has been on edge since we left the group. I talked with my father before we settled down to sleep. Letting him know that we would be heading over to the cabin to get another person.

My father isn't happy that we are splitting up, but we need to get Charlie. The snap of a stick pulls my attention to the other side of the river. I couldn't miss that scent. It is a bear, but it doesn't smell like a shifter. Glancing over to Georgie and Gracie, I realize that they are both frozen on the shore, watching the brown, huge bear on the other side.

The bear watches us, and I notice that its eyes shift differently than a regular bear's. Like it is more human than bear. But I couldn't understand how. Georgie slowly stands from her crouched position.

"Georgie!" I snarl under my breath. But she doesn't so much as look my way.

Chapter Seventeen

GEORGINNA

Standing there staring at the bear across from us and into the eyes of the one who has been a part of my life for so long. Those eyes give me comfort every time I look into them. Slowly rising, I hear Lang calling my name, but I cannot take my eyes off the bear.

I move forward, keeping my eyes on her, unable to look away. She sits, seeming to wait patiently for me. The rushing water brushes my legs as I cross the river. Luckily, it is shallow, so I make my way without issue.

Once on the other side, I pause. Might this possibly get me killed? Yes. Is this a great idea? No. But all sense goes away when I gaze into her eyes. The eyes that hold so much familiarity to me.

Is she a shifter? Is she someone I know? Why do I feel so comforted in her presence?

The bear steps closer. My breathing starts to shallow as she comes toward me. I hope my instincts are right this time. Adrenaline shoots through me with each inch she takes. Once she is within arm's length, I slowly reach for her. The feel of her fur is so soft through my fingers. Her fur seems to be the same color as my fur in my bear form. She leans into my touch, closing her eyes.

She steps back and she shifts into a beautiful, black-haired woman. Her features are eerily similar to mine.

"Aunt Aria?!" I hear Gracie shout from behind me. I look back to see Langdon, roughly five feet behind me, looking at me. Gracie stumbles forward.

Looking back at the woman, my knees give out. Before I hit the ground, Lang scoops me in his arms. "I got you," he whispers, kissing my forehead. All the air in me seems to vanish.

Can it really be her? That would explain the feelings I've been having whenever she is around. The reason for me being so comforted and safe. Is this really my mother?

"I am so sorry, my darling Georginna. I didn't mean to upset you. Everything that has happened in the last week have been tremendously upsetting. After you shifted for the first time, which I am so proud of you for, I felt it was time for us to reunite. Knowing you are safe now with your mate..."

I tap Lang's shoulder letting him know I need to stand. "Why did it take you so long? Why didn't you just come to me sooner?"

Lately, that's all I seem to have, more questions. Everything needs to slow the fuck down so I can catch up. Gracie steps forward and hands her some clothes.

"My sweet Grace. You both have grown so beautiful." She dresses quickly and takes my hands in hers. "I know you have many questions, but I plan on sitting down and catching up on everything. But from what I've heard, you all are heading north toward the Kodiaks ." She looks at Lang. He nods his approval, and she answers with a smile, returning her attention to me. "Then it is settled, I will be joining you."

These past couple of weeks have been so full of uncertainty and surprises. I am finished with all the surprises and ready to settle down and live a normal life with Langdon and our babies.

Did you know Mother was alive?

Although my bear is a part of me, I'm not entirely sure if she has the same memories as me. All of this is still new to me, I'm still learning so much about myself.

No, I didn't. I had a feeling the bear that has been with us was someone we knew; I had a strong sense that she was our mother. I wasn't going to say anything until I knew for a fact.

Langdon pulls me into his arms. "It will all be okay."

Resting my head on his chest, I take a deep breath. His scent brings me back to something familiar. With all the craziness and uncertainty around me, this is the one place that calms me.

"It's time to move out. We don't have much time. Gracie, are you certain you want Charlie with us, knowing where we're going and who we all are?" Gracie stands and nods.

"Yes, I'm sure. I'm going with my family. Charlie is a part of my family."

With that, we head out toward the cabin.

It feels like it's been forever since I was at this cabin. Being here on the porch, staring at the front entrance, I try to push the anxiety ripping at me away. The last time I was here, I was kidnapped.

Standing behind me, Lang places his hands on my shoulders. "I'm here with you. Nothing will happen to you as long as I live and breathe."

Reaching up, I take his hand in mine and lean into his chest. "I know." The quicker we go in and get Charlie, the sooner we can leave. This place no longer holds the safety and happiness I once felt, it's just a reminder of the shit that Garrett put me through.

My mother steps in front of me. "I'll stay out here and keep watch. I will alert you if there are any signs of movement."

I smile. "Thank you. We won't be too long."

"Okay, let's do this," I say as I head for the door. As soon as we walk in, I take in all of the cabin's disarray. Furniture knocked down from my struggle to get away from the men who kidnapped me, as well as books and papers that were thrown—all still in the same place as when I left. Moving into the kitchen, Charlie's blood still stains the floor. I take a staggering breath, reminding myself that he is alive and well.

"I'm going to talk to Charlie. Alone. I need to tell him who and what I really am. I'm hoping if he truly loves me, it won't matter," Gracie says, turning to me.

"Are you okay? I know it's hard being back here, considering what happened."

Nodding, I wrap her in a hug. "Yes, I'm good. Don't worry about me. It will all work out with you and Charlie. I've seen how much love he has for you. That kind of love only happens once in a lifetime." I smile at Langdon before turning back to Gracie.

"Even if it doesn't, know we are here for you. You have a family that will stick by you no matter what," I say as I rub my belly. "My babies will need their Auntie Grace to teach them to have fun and to love them." She smiles, then turns to Charlie's room.

"While we're here, I'm going to grab a few things." Langdon spins me around and kisses me. I laugh into his touch, enjoying his presence and surprised by his sudden change of mood. Wrapping my arms around his neck, I lean into him and deepen the kiss. His hands roam my curves. He lifts me into his arms and carries me to his room, not breaking the embrace.

Once we're in his room, he kicks the door shut, sets me on the bed, and crawls on top of me. I look up at him.

"Do we have enough time?" It comes out as a whisper. He smiles, and I lose all train of thought. I grab his neck pulling him into a deep kiss. His hands traverse my body until he reaches under my sweats, grazing my folds with the tips of his fingers.

"Mmm..." I moan, digging my fingers in his hair. He growls as I pull his hair and rubs my clit, igniting my body.

He trails his kisses to the spot just below my ear. The spot that sends tingles down to my core. I arch my chest up, meeting his as he continues his welcoming assault on my body. His hand leaves my swollen clit, and he stands, staring down at me and undoing his jeans, his eyes never leaving mine. He tears off my pants and panties, and without warning plunges into me, taking my breath away. I grip his shoulders, meeting him thrust for thrust as my body climbs higher and higher. "Come with me," he growls, and as if on cue, my orgasm hits its sweet assault.

As much as I would love to lie with him in post-coital bliss, we have so much to do.

A door opens down the hall, and I walk out to see Gracie and Charlie hand in hand. Gracie is smiling from ear to ear. It must've gone well. Although, Charlie looks a little worse for wear. Learning that not only that you were knocked unconscious and left for dead, but also that the love of your life is something you only hear about in stories would be taxing on anyone. He seems to be handling it better than I would.

"So, I see it went well." She nods.

"It was touch and go for a bit. He almost didn't believe me until I shifted in front of him. He almost fainted but kept his cool. It took some time for him to get used to the idea, but in the end, he said that he loves me no matter who I am."

Lovingly, I embrace her. I knew it would work out for the best.

"Now, all that's left is to pack what we need and hit the road." Langdon wraps his arms around my waist.

"I couldn't have said it better myself."

Chapter Eighteen

LANGDON

I stand on the porch, waiting for the others to finish packing. Glancing up at the darkening sky, the dampness of the forest tells me rain is getting closer. The smell of the rain always brings me back to when I was back in the tribal land.

It barely rains in Alaska. Giving us only sixty-seven inches of rain per year. So when it rained, I would play in it with the other cubs. The rain makes me feel refreshed.

Turning at the squeal of the door. Charlie comes out looking a little better than he did before. His eyes shift to me and then back out to the woods. I figure that he will be like this as it's all new to him. But he is going to have to get used to this if he is going to stay at the tribe.

"So, you're a bear too." I nod before turning to him.

Charlie isn't a small human, but he isn't as big as I am. "Yes, and there will be many more where we are going. Do you think you can handle that?"

"Yeah, as long as I've got Grace, then it will be okay. I think?" He runs his hands through his hair and grins.

"You'll be okay. There are other humans in the tribe, but they have been there for a long time."

Charlie nods and then rubs his hands against his shirt. I place my hand on his shoulder and sigh.

"It's going to be a long walk. We can't drive where we're going."

"Grace told me. I can make it." Another creak of the door brings our attention back toward the house. Georgie, Grace, and Georgie's mom come out, laughter proceeding them with backpacks full to bulging. Food will be caught along the way to minimize the rest of the weight.

"Are you ladies ready?"

"Yes." Georgie's eyes are brighter than ever before. All because her mother is now in her life.

"All right, well, let's go. It will take us a few days to get to the tribal lands. If we leave now, we might be able to beat my father there."

Everyone nods, and I turn to the forest just as the first drop falls from the sky. It is going to be one hell of a wet night.

The further north we go, the colder it is. My bear has been humming in excitement. It has been far too long since we have been home. Glancing behind me, Charlie is the only one who has a parka on. The cooler air on my skin is nothing less than amazing.

I can breathe better in the cooler air and the other three can as well. It is always way too hot in the lower states. The scent of bears in the air makes me realize that we are getting closer. There aren't many human towns the further away from the mainland.

Fortunately, we are able to find a charter bus to take us most of the way to Alaska. If we hadn't, it would have taken us a whole lot longer to get to my tribe. We still have to walk to the tribe's ferry because most humans here don't know we exist.

"How much longer till we get to the tribal land?" Charlie asks, breathing rapidly, the climb from the steep hill taking its toll on him

"Not much longer. We should see the first house shortly," I answer him while pointing ahead of us.

Since we are so close to the human civilization and have some living with us, we have built homes instead of tents. Even though we are solitary animals, our tribe is closer than any other. Just like the Rowans used to be.

Georgie is toward the back of our little pack, talking with Grace and her mom. As soon as I crest the hill, I spot the first house on the tribal land. We don't have cars since our land can provide for itself. So we don't need to go further inland to purchase things. Georgie, Grace, and Charlie will have to get used to how things are made around here.

Glancing around the tribal land, the wind picks up, welcoming me home. I make out the sparkling ocean in the distance. As much as I want to run to it and jump in, it isn't feasible right now. I have to get to the big house and tell my mother that I'm home and have brought new members.

Walking down the cobble-paved road, a few tribal members stare after us as we journey to the massive cabin near the ocean. More and more tribal members settle on the sidewalk, watching as we pass. I need to get to my parents' cabin and everything will be okay.

"Lang, why are they staring at us?" Georgie comes up to me and keeps my pace.

"Because they don't know you and haven't seen me in years." I glance at her and smirk before winking at her.

She nods, and we continue past the stores and more members. I recognize a few of the women who stand outside of the clothes shop and hardware store. Each of them looking the same as before I left. Though they look like they've been refurbished with new paint and roofs. Some of the small buildings have apartment-style homes above the stores. That way the owners don't have to go far and the town can continue to stay on the smaller side. Other homes were further in the forest that are more like huts. Those homes hold the families of the patrols and hunting parties.

We round the slight bend, and there it is. My childhood home. The one I ran away from because I didn't know if I could lead this tribe. But now that I have Georgie, I know that I will be able to. She just has to tell me if she wants to lead it with me. Because if she said she doesn't, we will leave and never come back.

I lead the small group up to the front doors and knock. Even though it is where I grew up, I haven't been here for years. The doors open, and Carson, the house steward, is there at the door. He is a little older, and his hair starting to turn gray.

Carson's face changes through a wild range of emotions. His mouth continues like he is a fish out of water before I hear her voice behind him.

"Carson, who is it? Don't just stand there, let them in."

My mother comes from the other end of the house. Leaning over Carson who backs away from the door. I grin at the same time she runs up to me, pulling me into a hug and spinning around.

"Langdon! When did you get here? Is your father here? Oh, my Goddess Artio! You have matured so much!" As I put her on her feet, she pinches my cheeks, examining me from head to toe.

"He should be here any day. Father had more bears to bring along than I did." Laughing, I turn and pull her under my arm "Mom, I want you to meet Georginna, her mother, and Grace. They are from the Rowan tribe. This is Charlie, Grace's mate."

"I had a feeling that you survived, Aria. If you hadn't, I knew that girl of yours would be alive. But no one would believe me. Looks like my Lang found you both." My mother steps forward just as Georgie's does, pulling Aria into an embrace before moving away.

"I'm so sorry for your loss, my friend. But you are welcome in our tribe."

I didn't realize that my mother and Aria were friends. Hell, I don't know much about her since she never really talks about the destruction of the Rowan tribe. She never really talks about her life before me and her taking over the tribe with my dad.

"Let's go and catch up in the sitting room." Georgie's mother nods and they both leave us.

"Well, let me show you guys to a room." I hold out my hand and Georgie takes it, Grace and Charlie following behind.

If my mother is one thing it is consistent. She never changes anything in the house; nothing can be out of place. She never gets angry, but it's always been clear when someone put something back wrong.

My parents' bedroom is at the end of the long, navy blue hall with extra rooms on this floor for those of a high-rank. Stopping at the first on my left, I open it and gesture to our guests.

"Grace, Charlie, you can stay here until my father arrives and decides otherwise." Nodding, they enter hand in hand.

"Come on, I'll show you my room," I say, pulling Georgie down the hall to my room.

I'm ready to take a shower and rest for a while. As soon as my father gets here, we will be interrogating the prisoners and then getting them ready for trial. I won't have the chance to rest again for a long time. I usher Georgie in and close the door. My room is the same as it was when I left. Its light gray walls are brightened with the sun's light coming from the vast window facing the ocean. The posters and sports items are flawless on their shelves. My bed is made, which isn't how I left it when I made my escape.

"This place is too neat to be a guy's room." Georgie giggles while walking around the room.

"Yeah, well, my mother made sure to keep it clean. It was messier than this when I lived here." I chuckle as I watch her finger the trophies on the shelves.

"You will have to show me around once everything is done." Georgie turns to me and grins.

I know what she is hinting at, but I need a shower, and I'm going to let her rest in the tub. She hadn't seen it yet, but I'm sure she is going to love it.

"Here, come on, I'll start you a bath, and you can relax for a while." I hook my finger toward her and open the door to my bathroom.

"O.M.G! Is that a claw-foot tub?" Georgie excitedly asks. Her hand goes to my arm as I step further into the room.

Reaching the tub, I turn on the water and go to the cabinets to find some body wash and shampoo.

Even though we bathed in the river on our journey, it didn't get us clean. Adjusting the water so that it isn't too hot for Georgie and the cubs, I place a stool beside it with a towel and the toiletries.

"Here, relax, and I'll be back once I have found something to eat for you. Okay?" She nods, and I pull her into my arms while placing a kiss to her forehead and cheeks.

I leave the room and go downstairs to the kitchen. When I get to the bottom of the stairs, the door to the house opens, and my father walks in. He looks tired and I know how he feels.

"Good, I was just wondering if you would make it here before me." He comes up to me and pats my shoulder.

"Yeah, you made great time with the number of prisoners you have."

"You know your old man doesn't like to be away from his tribe and his mate for very long." He steers me to the kitchen, and I allow him to. "I'm hungry. What has your mother cooked up?"

"I was just on my way there when you came in. Also, I wanted to let you know that I brought someone else with us." I glance out of the corner of my eye to watch his reaction,

His brows knit together as we open the kitchen doors. My father stops and grasps my shoulder. My mother and Georgie's turn to look at us, sipping glasses of wine.

"Aria? I thought you were dead."

Chapter Nineteen

GEORGINNA

I cannot believe I'm sitting in a claw-foot tub. It's always been my dream to have one. The water feels so good against my skin. The hot water soothing every tense muscle in my body. It's been too long since I had a bath. With everything that's happened in the last weeks, I don't remember the last time I was able to relax.

The trial comes to mind when I lean my head against the back of the tub.

How will they perform it? Is it in a courtroom with a judge, jury, and lawyers?

This is going to be interesting to see.

"You and your daddy are the best things that have happened to me this past year." I rub my belly. I cannot wait for these miracles to be here so I can hold them and show them how much they are loved.

It's been a crazy year. I found Langdon after losing him, I got kidnapped and found that I am not an ordinary person but a Kodiak bear shifter. Then, in a short amount of time, I found out I am pregnant with twins, and my birth mother is alive after everyone thought she was dead. All of this in a short two-month span.

The door creaks open, and Langdon steps inside, holding a bowl. I don't know what I would do without him. He is the best man I have ever known. When we're together, the world and all its shittiness fades away.

"Mother isn't finished with dinner yet, so I brought berries," he says, holding up the bowl before sitting on the stool and holding a berry out for me. "These are freshly picked. Mother went out foraging yesterday. Believe me, they will be the best you will ever taste."

I open my mouth, and as soon as the flavor hits my tongue, I close my eyes and savor the taste of the fresh berries. He was right. These are nothing like the ones back home. He holds out a yellow berry, similar to a raspberry, except this berry is yellow. I eat each delicious berry until the bowl is empty.

After setting the bowl on the counter by the sink, he sits on the stool and picks up the shampoo, squirting it in his hands.

"Sit back," he orders, and I do. Rubbing his hands together, he starts massaging the soap into my scalp. A moan escapes me as I close my eyes, enjoying the feel of his hands caressing my head. He rubs in small circles deliciously slow; I take in the sensations. I've never been this taken care of by someone who wasn't my mom. The way Lang takes care of me gives me hope that he will make a fantastic father.

"Now, sit up so I can rinse you off." Again, I do as instructed. He grabs a cup, fills it with water, and pours it over my head. The feel of the water on my scalp sends warmth throughout my entire body. With his other hand, he scrubs the suds out, taking his time as he does.

Once my hair is clean, he grabs a washcloth and shower gel. "Sit back for me and lift your legs."

He grabs the stool and moves it to the other end of the tub, where my feet are. I do as he asks. He starts at my toes, lathering them up, then takes his time washing each toe. Leaning my head back, I revel in the love this man is showing me as he moves higher up my leg and then moves to the next. He continues the same way, starting at my feet and moving slowly upward. Stopping at my upper thighs, he moves the stool to the side of the tub.

How could a man as hot and strong as Langdon be this gentle and loving? How did I get so lucky?

He is everything I have ever wanted. Someone who not only loves me but cares for me so gently and satisfies every need and desire. Never in my life have I imagined living the life I am. Having a family I never knew existed and creating one of my own. Life has surely done a one-eighty this past year. I don't think I could ever turn back, even if I wanted to.

"Stand for me. It's time for your upper body." As always, I do as he says. He continues slowly, and I savor every lathery touch as he washes from my neck down.

As he gets to my lower abdomen, he pauses and then looks up at me, a smile forming on his lips. He continues and starts cleaning between my legs, working even slower until he gets to my folds.

Licking his lips, he encircles my clit before plunging two fingers inside my pussy. It doesn't take too long before my knees start to give out. He stops and catches me, setting me in the water.

"Easy, beautiful." He smiles and continues what he started. His fingers start moving in and out of me, the water moving simultaneously. The sensation in me climbs higher and higher as he moves. The orgasm builds but doesn't come.

"Oh God!" I shout as my body starts to shake. I grip the sides of the tub, trying to chase the orgasm that is so close yet so far. "Come for me, beautiful." His words are my undoing. I explode in ecstasy, my body spasming as he removes his fingers. He leans down and kisses me as I wrap my hands around his head, deepening the kiss.

After an amazing afternoon of the best sex of my life, I fell asleep. I feel well-rested and relaxed. A feeling I haven't felt in so long. I look over beside me and Langdon isn't there. Swinging my legs over the side of the bed, I grab my clothes and head for the bathroom.

Walking downstairs, I hear voices. It sounds like everyone is gathered, and Langdon didn't bother to wake me. He looks over at me as I step into the living room. Walking over, he wraps his arm around my waist.

"Why didn't you wake me when you got up?" I whisper.

He smiles and leans down so close to my ear that I can feel his breath, sending chills over my body. "You were sleeping so peacefully, I didn't want to wake you. We're just catching up. You didn't miss anything." He kisses my neck and stands.

Langdon's mother walks over to me and holds her hands out. I smile and unwrap myself from him, placing my hands in hers.

"You are so beautiful. I am so happy my Langdon found you."

I can't help but blush at her compliment. "Thank you. If you don't mind me asking, how do you know my mother?"

She guides me to the couch and the three of us sit together, her hand staying in mine the whole time.

"We have been friends since we were kids. We grew up together. We grew older, married, and went our separate ways. She went to the tribe that her husband led, and I stayed here where my husband was. After I heard about the horrible massacre, I feared she had died. I went to check, but the only thing to see was the gruesome aftermath. After what I saw, I believed she hadn't made it. I have never been so glad to be wrong."

She looks over and smiles at my mother. That's still a lot to get used to, 'Mother'. For some reason, it feels right to call her my mother. It feels like she's always been with me. Well, I guess she has, in a way.

"I'm Olivia, by the way. I am so happy my boy found someone as wonderful as you," she says, looking back at me and wrapping me in a hug.

"It's nice to meet you. Langdon is a wonderful man. I'm glad he came into my life." I grab his hand and squeeze, smiling up at him.

Archer stands. "We need to discuss the plans for tomorrow's trial. Of course, my dear Olivia will be by my side."

I look around the room, and there are five people I didn't see arrive.

"My son Langdon and his mate Georginna will also be at my side. These animals have disgraced the bear population and have killed our fellow Kodiaks. Before sentencing them, we are going to find out why they have massacred the Rowan tribe and bring them to justice." He looks over at my mother and then at me.

"We will work to restore what has been broken. You are more than welcome here for as long as you like." He walks over to me and holds a hand out. I take it and stand next to him. "You are a part of our family now and will be treated as such. My son could not have found a more suitable mate."

I smile in response and resume my place next to Lang.

※ ※ ※

We stand in front of a grassy field with Kodiaks surrounding us in a huge circle, ensuring the prisoners cannot escape. Archer steps into the center and clears his throat. "It is time for the trial to begin. We will start by bringing our first prisoner forward." He waves a hand toward Garrett.

Garrett moves forward with encouragement from the guards. "First things first, state your name." Garrett stands there, his head up and jaw clenched. It doesn't seem like he's going to be very forthcoming.

A guard hits him with a stick, knocking him to his knees. "You *will* answer when asked a question." The guard's eyes glows bright amber, making Garrett cower. He took a deep breath and stands once more. "Garrett Graves."

Archer nods. "Now tell us, Garrett Graves, why did your tribe target the Rowans?"

I lean in to listen. This has been weighing on me since he kidnapped me. *Why me? Why my family?*

Garrett smirks at me and then back at Archer. "It all started with a treaty between Chief Mateo and Ezra Rowan. It stated that Chief Mateo would have the first-born cub in exchange for peace between the tribes. Ezra accepted and when the cub was born..." He glares at me. "...Ezra backed out of the deal. Chief Mateo was not too happy to be betrayed, so he executed the Rowan tribe for treachery."

Langdon grabs my hand and squeezes. Rage rises within me. How can people be so cold? To trade others off as though they are property.

Why would my father agree to something like that? Was I the one that he was going to trade for? This is something I need to talk to my mother about.

Garrett didn't have to say it. I know it was me they were after. I was the one that was offered to Mateo. That is all I needed to hear.

The rest of the trial continued in the same vibe. Archer asks each one their name and their side of the story. They were loyal to Mateo to a fault.

From day one, it had been carved into their heads that the Kodiaks were the enemy. I don't believe that for a second. From the research I have done and from what I have learned recently from my new family, the Kodiaks are a peaceful tribe.

Once the trial comes to a close, the Grizzly prisoners are sent off to be executed. Although I *do* see why, I'm not sure about putting anyone to death. I've always believed that jail and prison are the best way, but if I want to sleep better at night, things are going to have to change.

Chapter Twenty

LANGDON

After the trial, my mother and Georgie suggested we have a bonding ceremony. My father has been talking with me about taking over now that I have found my mate. Although, I still needed to talk to Georgie about it since she will be the female chief.

Georgie and I agree with them that the bonding ceremony is an excellent way to strengthen our bond. Allowing our bears and our human form to feel the other will be so much better than what we have now.

Once we agreed, our mothers went full swing into getting everything for the event.

I stand in the sitting room, watching the other members of the tribe put up decorations displaying the tribe's colors. Flags, paper lanterns, and string lights hang from tree to tree.

Another set of members is building a large fire pit on the beach in the middle of tiered seats. The smell of the cedar that will be burned later today hangs in the air.

My heart is slowly starting to race as I observe everything being put together. I'm not nervous about bonding with Georgie. She is my mate, and soon, our cubs will arrive. So, having the bonding ceremony now will be more beneficial as it will allow us to be stronger together. The only thing I'm worried about is that Georgie won't want to lead this tribe with me.

And if that happens, I will heed her decision and follow her back to the continental states if I have to. I'm not going to be without her again, especially with her carrying my babies.

"So, has the pike been swimming in your stomach?" I turn to see my father coming to stand next to me.

"Yes, how did you know you and Mom were ready to take over the tribe?"

"To tell you the truth. You're never ready. You have to take it and know that you have a strong mate to help you with everything."

I take a deep breath and run my hand through my hair. Glancing over to my father, I can now see why people always told me that I'm his twin. We both have a brown beard and mustache, but his is thicker than mine with a little grey splashed in his. Our eyes are the same color and shape.

My father has always been my hero even when he was teaching me hard lessons. Even though he didn't like that I had left without getting my bear, he allowed me to make my own choices. Something I hope that I will be able to do for my kids.

"Your mother told me about the cubs. Are you excited?"

"Yeah, it's crazy to be having twins."

"Well, they are in our line. I'm sure they run in Georginna's line. Her mother is a twin."

Most of the bears have twins; some even have triplets. I once knew a female in our tribe with five, but that is just out of the ordinary. One of her cubs was my best friend before I left for the States.

"It's going to be a wild ride. I do know that much." I laugh as we continue to watch everyone prepare for the festivities.

Many are in groups, building things and making items for the tables. It always amazes me how the tribe pulls together for events. It literally takes a village to run this tribe. Even though it is mainly on the shoulders of the Chief and his Chieftess.

But at the end of the day, it takes all of us to help each other and take care of the cubs. Being gone and returning to my tribe has made me realize that I haven't been looking for somewhere else to put down roots.

I was called to the States to find Georgie, my mate and not only to bring her home but Gracie and Aria as well. Because in my heart, I knew that I had a mission. I just didn't know what it was until it all happened.

"I'm proud of you, Langdon."

Turning to my father, I notice the uptick of his lip in the corner. My father has always been my hero, and I know that at some point in my life, I let him down. But this is the first time that he has actually told me that he is proud of me.

"Thanks, Dad. You know I wouldn't be the bear I am if it wasn't for you."

He chuckles and turns to me, bringing me to face him. "Son, as much as I want to believe that, it's not true. You have always been a fighter and understood when to stand up for yourself and others. That trait was with you even before you could see. You are going to make one hell of a leader. The both of you."

I nod; I want to take over and make my father even prouder than he is at this moment. But if Georgie doesn't want to assume her position as chieftess, then I won't force her. I need to talk to Georgie about it because it all depends on her decision.

"Let's get you dressed up and ready for your bonding ceremony. We have to make sure you look great for your mate." I laugh with him, and we walk over to one of the rooms.

It is a tradition that the male is shown off in front of his mate. To allow her to realize that she is choosing the right male, even though it is the goddess's will. If I'm being honest, I was excited that it is my time to have my bonding.

I'm dressed in traditional white breechcloths and no shirt, as is customary. The older men draw the spiritual symbols on my arms. I spot one of the elders mixing the iron oxides, roots, berries, beets, and ochre into red paint in a wooden bowl. He has been doing this for years, and now it is my turn.

He comes up to me and places the wooden bowl in front of me on a stool. He smiles a toothless grin and plunges his hands into the scarlet paint. Pulling them out, he fists them in the shape of a bear's paw and places both onto my chest. After, he makes five claw marks above the paws.

"It has been a long time coming for this day, young chief. I'm happy that I'm the one to bond with you today."

"Thank you, it has been a long time. I'm glad that I've found my mate."

"I knew you would. When you left, I knew you would be back." The Elder's smile widens before he walks away to wash his hands.

The wind brings the scent of cedar over to the cabin. The fire for the ceremony has been lit. The bonding ceremony is getting closer, and by the time the sun sets over the sea, Georgie and I will be a bonded pair.

Walking out of the cabin, I stop to scan the decorations. Even though I watched the other tribe members set them up, I still take a moment to enjoy everything. Members line the street to the beach with candles in the waning light.

I walk out and down to the beach and the fire pit and the seats. The men that line the streets follow behind me, chanting. My bear inside me sways with the chants as we continue down the street. We couldn't have picked a better day for the ceremony. Once I get to the beach, I walk out to the water, waiting for Georgie to make her way to me. A few people are already filing into the seats behind me.

The drums start up, causing my heart to race. This is the signal that Georgie is on her way to me. As she walks, she is followed by the women chanting behind her.

A burst of wind brings Georgie's scent to me. They have bathed her in the ceremonial bath soaps, which I have always loved. It is a gift to the Goddess Artio, who is sharing it with me on the wind.

The Elder comes up to me and motions for me to turn. When I do, I think that the Goddess Artio herself is before me. Georgie is stunning in her traditional white dress. Her hair was in braids, and the paint tattoos on her face give her a glow.

Animal fur adorns her shoulders, and the warm animal skin dress keeps her from chilling. The naturally-dyed colors on the clothing are starting to fade. The dress I notice is my mother's; I saw it when I was younger. She had hoped to have a daughter to pass it down to. To watch her bond with her mate, but she had only me.

Holding out my hands to Georgie, she slips them into mine. Turning us to the Elder, I try to calm my heart, but I can't stop looking at my gorgeous mate.

"Kodiak tribe! We are here to bond these two young bears together. They have been through much and now have decided to give themselves to each other and the Goddess Artio." We both stay quiet as he glances behind him and nods. Another bear comes up, bringing a long cloth with them. Stitched into the ends are a human and bear, along with ceremonial symbols.

"Turn and hold hands." We do as he directs, and the Elder starts to chant in our old tongue as he wraps the cloth around our hands and allows the ends to hang.

The pull from my bear's soul begins as the chanting becomes louder. It is like something is sitting on my shoulders and chest. I never take my eyes away from Georgie. Once the Elder's voice starts to lower, I feel the snap as we become one.

I lower my forehead to touch hers so that I can breathe in her scent. "Georgie, I need to know. Will you help me lead this tribe and become my chieftess?"

Georgie's eyes search mine, tears pooling, threatening to fall.

"Yes."

Epilogue

Georginna

One Year Later

I cannot believe how fast the year has passed by. One minute, I'm bonding with my mate, and the next, I'm sitting on the beach watching my two beautiful kids running around chasing each other. It is crazy how fast they've grown. The pregnancy was shorter than any normal human pregnancy. In just six short months, Ella and Liam arrived and brightened my world. Although I had a scare, everything turned out great.

"You can do this, Georgie. I am here with you," Lang encourages as I try and push for the umpteenth time. This baby doesn't want to come. The first one came no problem, my sweet girl.

"One last push." the doctor says as I take a deep breath and push,

"Ughhhh…" I push as much as I can until finally, he arrives.

"It's a boy!" The doctor shouts. Langdon takes my hand and kisses the top of my head. "Thank you for this beautiful gift. You did amazing." The doctor turns and cleans my son up. Langdon turns to him before taking both of our beautiful babies and handing them to me.

He placed each of them in the creases of each of my arms.

"What are their names?" a nurse asks. I look at the beautiful babies.

"Ella and Liam." They both open their eyes and look up. My eyes widen, and my brows knit together. Their eyes are almost white, and they seem to be looking side to side. My breath quickens.

"Georgie? What's wrong?" Langdon asks as he places his hand on my shoulder. I look up at him, tears staining my cheeks.

"Are they blind?"

How? Why? I did everything I could to follow the strict orders given to me by the doctors. Langdon looks at me, clearly relieved. How is he smiling now? Something seems to be wrong with our babies, and he doesn't seem to care.

"They are fine. It is normal for cubs to be blind when they are born." He touches my cheek, and I lean into his touch, then look up at him.

"How long does it last?" I try to keep the terror out of my voice. "Usually for about a month. In that time, you will stay with them, feed them, and care for them."

A month?! My poor babies will not be able to see for a month?

Looking down at them, I hold them tighter and kiss the top of their heads. This will be a tough four weeks...

It all worked out. I breastfed Ella and Liam for that month, and when their eyes cleared, I was astounded. Ella has Langdon's beautiful green eyes, and Liam has my baby blue eyes. Of course, both of them are brunette, just like their father.

I can't believe that after all this time, we are finally happy. When Langdon asked me to lead the tribe at his side, I was scared. I'd never led anything before, let alone a tribe.

However, now that I have the two most precious beings and Langdon with me, the fear has faded, and in its place is pure joy. "Mommy, look what I found!" Ella exclaims as she brings me something clenched in her hands.

"What is it?" She opens her hand to reveal a heart-shaped shell. "I found the best shell for you."

I pick her up and wrap her in a hug. "I love it! Thank you, my sweet girl." I kiss the top of her head, and she runs back toward Liam.

"They are amazing children," Langdon says as he grabs my waist and spins me around, surprising me.

Smiling up at him, I say, "I think so, too." Resting my head on his chest, we stand there swaying as we watch our cubs play.

In the span of two years, we had gone through a terrifying emotional rollercoaster. Now I am finally with the love of my life and two amazing children, who have grown so big so fast.

Also By C.L. Ledford

Paranormal Romance

The Second Alpha Heir

The Fallen Alpha

Silver Moon Kiss

Silver Moon Kiss: Becoming Alpha

Contemporary Romance

Raising the Stakes: A Dark CEO Romance

Craving the Taboo: A Dark Forbidden Romance

About C. L. Ledford

C. L. Ledford was born in the city of Chattanooga, TN. Where she was raised by her grandparents, to be a strong and independent person. She became an avid reader at the age of eleven, when her fifth grade teacher gifted her the book, The Black Stallion. With this book her love of books grew. In middle school she began to write what would be one of many books swirling around in her head. Silver Moon Kiss came to life with two chapters and multiple scenes before it was packed away and not thought of until after she had become an adult. C. L. Ledford writes in Paranormal Romance and Contemporary Romance. Her first published book The Second Alpha Heir released on June 14, 2022.

By this time she had moved to a little town called Ringgold, GA and married her husband where they raise their three children and five German Shorthair dogs. Along with her love of writing and reading, she also enjoys hunting behind her dogs.

Also By J. L. Hinds

Once Upon A Quill (A Quill Lost in Time Book 1)

Curse of the Quill (A Quill Lost in Time Book 2)

The One

About J. L. Hinds

J.L. moved to Dalton, Georgia from the small town of Reeds Spring, Missouri. She was born in Watsonville, California and lived in Santa Cruz until the age of seven. J.L. developed the love of writing through her love of reading. She got inspired to write by her favorite author, Heather Graham, through her stories. The way she writes inspired J.L. to write her own stories and entertain people, to draw on their imaginations and to bring different worlds of fiction to the readers. She wanted to give readers the same excitement she gets from books.

Milton Keynes UK
Ingram Content Group UK Ltd.
UKHW020814231024
450026UK00004B/217

9 798218 520236